CRAZY WEEKEND

GARY SOTO

AN
APPLE
PAPERBACK

SCHOLASTIC INC.
New York Toronto London Auckland Sydney

RETA E. KING LIBRARY
CHADRON STATE COLLEGE
CHADRON, NE 69337

ISBN 0-590-47076-0

Copyright © 1994 by Gary Soto.
All rights reserved. Published by Scholastic Inc.
APPLE PAPERBACKS is a registered trademark of Scholastic Inc.

12 11 10 9 8 7 6 5 4 3 2   3   5 6 7 8 9/9 0/0

Printed in the U.S.A.   40

To Jeff Knight

CHAPTER 1

Hector Beltran and his *carnal* Mando Tafolla, both seventh-graders from East Los Angeles, stepped off the train. Each held a suitcase in one hand and their shoulders were weighed down with backpacks. It was February, cold, and fog had smothered Fresno like a white shroud. Fog hung between the telephone lines and over parked cars and trucks. Fog dimmed the traffic lights. Fog blew down the empty streets of the Santa Fe depot. Fog lived in the very bones of each passenger who stepped off the train.

"*Hace mucho frío*," Mando said as he dropped his suitcases and rubbed his cold hands. He was tall for a boy of thirteen, with hair the color of wet coal. "Where's your *tío*?"

"*No sé*," Hector said, straining to see through the fog. He put down his suitcase and breathed into his hands, which were pink as the underside of a starfish. Like Mando, he was tall, with thick, black hair, and beneath his clothes, his body was hardened with muscle from playing sports, mostly soccer.

The two boys had been sent to Fresno for a three-day weekend, an idea spawned by Hector's mother, who said they should see another part of the world.

"You and Mando should travel," Hector's mother suggested one night when she saw that they were so bored they were counting the hairs on their knuckles and arguing about who had more.

Hector had imagined Paris or Madrid, and Mando had imagined Acapulco where he could take a blow-up raft and ride the large white-tipped waves until they sputtered into fingers of foam. They saw themselves sporting sunglasses propped on their heads. They saw themselves asking for directions, and then giving directions. They saw themselves eating in fancy restaurants with white napkins under their chins.

That was in October, when a few herds of leaves were scuttling through the streets in "East Los." Now it was February, and they were standing like two lone birds at the train station waiting for Hector's uncle, Julio, a photographer. Hector hadn't seen him in two years, since the time Uncle Julio visited and treated him to Disneyland. Later they rented two surfboards to crack the waves at Malibu Beach. Neither of them was any good at surfing, but the crashing waves worked up an appetite that was solved by a huge dinner on Olvera Street.

Hector and Mando were looking nervously at each other, wondering if anyone would pick them up when they heard through the fog, "Hey, you little *vatos*."

Hector and Mando turned to see a man approach them with two cameras hanging on his shoulders. He was tall, mustached, and walking with a cane. He had a kind face, and was dressed casually in khakis and an overcoat. He resembled a detective, rumpled and a bit worn.

"You've grown," Uncle Julio said, ruffling Hector's hair.

"It's Mom's cooking!" Hector said with a smile. "What happened to your leg?"

"I fell out of an airplane." He hooked the cane in the crook of his arm and gave his nephew a hug.

"An airplane!" Hector said with surprise.

"The airplane was parked. On the ground. And lucky for me, 'cause I wasn't wearing a parachute." He shrugged one of the cameras off his shoulder and took off the lens cap. "This is your *amigo* Mando?"

"Yeah, this is Mando."

"Hey, Mando, welcome," the uncle said. They shook hands *raza* style.

"*Mucho gusto*, Mr. Silva. Me and Hector are glad you're gonna let us stay with you."

"No problem. Call me Julio, Mando," Uncle said. He raised one of his cameras to his eye and snapped the shutter. The lens blinked at them three times before Uncle capped the lens and shrugged the camera back onto his shoulder. He took a suitcase from Hector. "So how was the trip?"

"Long," Hector answered. "We saw nothin' but fog."

"We saw a crash," Mando interrupted.

"Nah, Mando, the guy was just parked weird."

"Nah, I saw his front fender. It was all smashed up."

"That was an ole' wreck. You need glasses."

"You're the one who needs glasses!"

The two argued as they left the train station. They got into Uncle's Ford Escort station wagon and cooled their argument as the car started through the fog that would claim Fresno until a wind blew it away, or a cloud let loose its cargo of rain.

"You still taking pictures, Uncle?" Hector asked after a while. A cold shudder ran up Hector's back as the car's warm air stirred among them.

When Julio was in the Air Force, he had

learned photography. He kept busy snapping pictures of generals and colonels, and wreckage of jets that went down, mostly from mechanical problems but sometimes from pilot error. After he got out of the service, he worked in Los Angeles for a popular magazine. He decided to move from L.A. when the smog and traffic worked on his nerves. He was also being pestered by an old girlfriend, and the girlfriend's new boyfriend, a man with tattoos of snakes that slithered down his arm.

"That's my job. That's what I do," Uncle said. He hit the radio with the flat of his palm, and country music started to vibrate from the speaker. "I'm going to take you to work with me right now."

"Where?" Hector asked.

"You'll see." Uncle flicked on the windshield wipers, which cleared away the mist.

They drove from Fresno to an orange grove. Uncle stopped the car and put on the emergency blinkers. The three of them piled out of the car and, camera raised, Uncle took a rapid succession of pictures of a tree that was knocked down. Its trunk was split and the white meat of tree flesh showed.

"Why are you taking pictures of the tree?" Hector asked.

"A guy got drunk and ran into it. Believe it

or not, a tree like this is *mucho dinero*."

"You get paid for taking pictures of orange trees?" Mando asked. He was confused. He thought that photographers only took pictures of brides, families, and cute babies with sausage-like arms and legs.

"Yeah, that's my job, that's what I do," Uncle answered. He pulled two oranges from the fallen tree and tossed them to Hector and Mando, who clawed their fingers into the skin. Then Uncle plucked three more oranges and started juggling them. "I learned this in the Air Force, too." The oranges stayed in the air for a few seconds before dropping into the mud. Breathing hard but feeling good, Uncle quipped, "If the photography biz ever gets really lousy, I'll join the circus."

From the orange grove, they returned to town and Uncle's apartment over a garage. The garage held three cars that belonged to Uncle's landlord, a chiropractor. Sometimes they traded services. Uncle would take pictures of the chiropractor's patients, and the doctor would crack and realign Uncle's spine.

The boys piled out, happy that they had finally arrived.

"Wow, Uncle Julio, you got a nice crib," Hector said, jerking his head at the low ranch style house.

"Nah, that's Dr. Femur's place. I live over the

garage," Uncle said, pointing his cane at the two-story structure.

Hector shrugged. They climbed the steps to the apartment, with Uncle in tow. He moved slowly with his hurt leg, cane tapping the ground.

"This is where you guys are gonna stay," Uncle said. With his cane, he pointed to the couch. "It pulls out."

Hector put down his suitcases and looked around the apartment, which held a brown couch, brown chairs, brown desk and lamp, and a brown-looking cat sleeping by the heater. The cat raised its head and blinked its sleepy eyes at the boys.

"I guess you like brown, Mr. Silva," Mando said. He looked down at his blue pants, then fingered the cuffs of his shirt. It was blue. "I like blue, I guess."

"Actually, this is the furniture my ex-wife left," Uncle said. "I'm divorced." His mustache lifted in a smile.

"Uncle, Mom said that I should give this to you."

"Is that right?" Uncle said.

Hector bent down, unlocked the suitcase, and it sprang open like a jack-in-the-box. Wrapped in a pair of faded corduroy bell-bottoms were phonograph records from the 60's and 70's —

Santana, Otis Redding, The Chamber Brothers, The Stones . . .

"Oh, wow, my records!" Uncle yelled happily. He told Hector, "Your Mom was always stealing my records and taking them to parties. I finally get them back."

"Mom was a party animal?"

"*Pues sí.* She was a frisky girl. A filly."

Hector couldn't quite picture his mother dancing at a party. To Hector, she seemed conservative. She was always complaining about his rap music.

Uncle took one record from its worn album cover. Santana. He grimaced. "It's all scratched. And what's this stuff? Looks like peanut butter." He rubbed his thumb over some caked food and flakes fell like snow.

When the telephone rang, Uncle tossed the record album on the couch and answered it. "I'm telling you," he said into the receiver, "Rick don't live here." He looked at the boys, the phone in the crook of his neck. He whispered, "Crank call. I think it's my ex-roommate's girlfriend."

He hung up, giggling. He returned to the suitcase. He hoisted a pair of bell-bottom pants to his waist. "They might still fit."

"Uncle, you wore these?" a startled Hector asked.

8

"That was the style, *ese*," Uncle said. He tossed the pants on the couch. "I'll show you two." He pointed to the bulletin board in the kitchen. They walked over and Hector and Mando gazed at a creased snapshot. It was a group of college students with raised fists of defiance.

"That was when I was in *MEChA*," Uncle explained. "That's me, a groovy *Mechista*." He poked a finger at a guy with long hair and sunglasses.

"That was you, Uncle?" Hector asked in disbelief. "Wow, you look like a criminal."

"Hey, man, I was radical. I was a heavy-duty *Chicano*. Still am, *ese*. I even got a Mexican flag hanging in the bedroom." He had to laugh at his nephew's comment. He had to laugh at himself. He did have long hair and an angry look on his face. "Come on, let's eat."

That first night they grubbed on canned soup and tuna on hard bread. They shared one puny tomato. They also shared a thorny pickle floating in cloudy juice. For dessert, they had candy and oranges from the tree that was struck and left for dead. Uncle then said, "I'm gonna teach you *vatos* how to make the best salad in all of Fresno. Betty Crocker don't know this recipe."

"A salad?" Mando asked.

"*Simón*," Uncle answered.

9

Hector shrugged his shoulders and said, "Okay."

"It's more than 'okay,' homes. It's good for you."

They prepared what Uncle called the Super Bowl salad. He buttered a large bowl and pressed peas around the sides into neat rows: these were the spectators. Then he leveled the bottom with cottage cheese: this was the snowy playing field. He added toothpicks for the goals and black and green olives for the teams. The cherries were cheerleaders. The peppercorns were referees. The football was an olive pit.

"¡Órale!" Uncle said. He wiped his hands on a dish towel and, stepping back and arms out, bragged, "Check it out!"

"Where did you learn how to make this?" Hector asked.

"College, of course. We'll eat it tomorrow. Let's get ready for bed."

Hector showered first, then Mando. Uncle flipped out the bed. Inside was an old magazine, a broken pencil, and a gym sock. He slapped them away and smoothed the brown-printed sheets. "Let's hit the sack."

Hector and Mando rolled into bed.

"Ouch," Hector complained. A spring pushed into the small of his back. "This bed hurts."

"Simón," Mando agreed. "I think I hurt my pitching arm."

They rolled toward the center. They pushed each other and Mando yelled, "Gimme some room. You're hogging all the space."

"You're taking it all. Give me my pillow back."

"It's my pillow, Hector."

All night they flopped like fishes from back to stomach. They couldn't find a perfect position. It was the first of two nights of fitful sleep.

CHAPTER 2

The next morning Uncle Julio threw together a breakfast of *huevos con weenies*. While he worked, he whistled through his mustache and then yelled, "Get up, lazy bones," as he flung a tortilla onto the burner. He opened the refrigerator and brought out a plastic jug of milk. He examined the half-empty jug closely and saw that the milk was six days beyond its expiration date. Still, he poured them each a glass, figuring that they were young blood who would get over it if they got sick.

Hector and Mando stirred from bed, each massaging the small of his back where a spark of pain throbbed. They kicked the blankets off and got up, hobbling like old men.

"I feel like I got tackled by Bertha Sanchez," Mando complained. Bertha was one of the baddest fighters at school. She could throw a boy's face into the grass and then get mad because his fall crushed it.

"I'm gonna use Uncle's cane," Hector joked.

He looked around and saw that the cane was hooked on the oven door, within reach of his uncle.

They sat down at the kitchen table and read the sports page together. While the boys ate, Uncle limped to the window and looked out. The fog had cleared. A patch of blue hovered in the east, where a sliver of sun shone.

"I got a shoot today," he announced as he turned from the window to face the boys, who were draining the milk in their glasses. "I want you guys to come along."

Uncle went into his bedroom where he packed his camera, a Nikon, and tossed rolls of fresh film into his shoulder bag.

Hector folded the bed and picked up while Mando did the dishes with his sleeves rolled up. A beard of soap suds clung to his elbows, flattening the boyish hairs on his arms.

"Let's go. *Ándale,*" Uncle said, after the boys had dressed.

The three of them climbed into the car. Uncle started the engine, which groaned and coughed before its four cylinders rocked to life. He revved the engine. He turned on the heater, which threw out a gust of cold air that would soon turn warm. He banged on the radio, and once again country music — George Strait — twanged from the cracked speaker.

"You like country music?" Hector asked.

"That's all the radio plays."

"*¿De veras?*" Mando said with surprise. He played with the dial. No matter where the indicator moved, the station wouldn't change. All it played was a country song about a broken-down truck and a wife moving out on the sly.

Mando and Hector exchanged looks that said, "The music's sorry."

They stopped for gas and air for their right rear tire. They then drove west until the city gave way to stinky dairy farms where cows grazed, staring dully at the ground. They arrived at a small airport with a line of single-propeller planes. It looked deserted. Some of the runway lights were blown out, dead. A herd of tumbleweed clung to the sides of the hangar, and the firetruck held no more than a ladder and a fire extinguisher. The truck's tires looked flat.

Hector peered out the window at the airport. He asked, "What kind of job do you have, Uncle?"

"I'm gonna take a picture of a farm."

"But this is the airport," Hector said, his head tilted in confusion.

"You'll see."

The car stopped and the three of them climbed out. The day was blustery. Two flags were whipping like laundry. The chain link fence was rattling, and a line of blackbirds huddled on a telephone wire. The three of them hurried toward the hangar, where a man in an orange coat was striking a plane's landing gear with a large wrench. He stood up when he saw the three of them coming and turned down a radio that was playing country-western.

"Hey, Stewart," Uncle greeted.

"Hey, Julio. How's the leg?"

"Stiff but in one piece. I picked up this stick over at Salvation Army." He tapped the cane on the wing of the airplane.

"I'm sorry that you fell off the plane. It's slippery sometimes — like now."

"It's part of the biz," Uncle said as he looked skyward. "We have to shoot the Inouye spread in Parlier if you think we can get up."

"I don't see a problem," Stewart said. He banged on the landing gear and asked, "Who are these young bloods?"

"My nephew Hector and his friend Mando. They're from Los Angeles. They're staying until my cooking kills them."

"Your sofa bed may kill us first," Hector quipped.

"That's for sure," Mando agreed.

Stewart chuckled and said, "Let me grab my log book and we'll go."

Only after Stewart was out of sight did Hector

ask, "We're not going to get in this thing, are we?" He jerked a thumb at the airplane. The silvery paint was faded and flaking. He touched a hole where a rivet had once been. The side window had a crack, and when Hector looked he saw that the seats were ripped and the stuffing was coming out.

"Stewart's great," Uncle reassured. "He could fly a truck."

"Can't we just drive? It's safer," Mando said.

"I gotta shoot a farm from the air," Uncle said. He explained that farmers took pictures of their ranches, just like people took pictures of their family. To do this, he said, he teamed up with Stewart and they had yet to crash the plane. For six hundred dollars, plus fuel for the plane, they would buzz a farm and snap a picture. Usually, the farmer, when he heard the plane coming, would get onto his tractor and pretend to work. His wife and children would stand in the dirt driveway and wave. Even the dogs would get into the act by barking and pulling on their chains.

Stewart returned to the hangar with a box of donuts. His log book was pinched between his arm and chest.

All four of them climbed into the little airplane, a Cessna 143, with Hector and Mando squished in the back. Immediately, Hector looked around for a parachute. He made a pained face. To his dismay, instead of finding a parachute he discovered a rust hole. He wiggled his finger into the hole, worm-like, and showed Mando, who crossed himself and mumbled a prayer.

Stewart pressed the starter and the propeller churned slowly until the engine sneezed, sputtered, and finally came alive. He put on a pair of ratty gloves. He put on a pair of sunglasses. He gave a thumbs-up sign and muttered, "Come on, baby," to his plane.

Hector looked at Mando, big-eyed with uncertainty. He asked, "You scared?"

"Yeah," Mando said, squirming in his seat as the Cessna fishtailed onto the runway and Stewart gunned the engine. The plane rolled down the strip and lifted with a bounce and a sway. Hector held back a scream. He closed his eyes, and when he opened them, he saw the blue sky in front of him and Stewart nibbling on a donut. He wasn't even looking at where he was flying.

Uncle took out his Nikon and adjusted the f-stop. He took out a lens as tall as a thermos. He fixed it onto the camera, and then brought out a map that he studied. He turned to Stewart and yelled over the engine roar, "It's on Manning and Central. The Inouye farm."

Stewart nodded his head and passed the donuts to Hector and Mando, who took them and laid them in their laps. Any other time, they would have glued their faces to that sweetness. But now, they had other things on their minds.

The Cessna banked and slowed to a hover. Uncle opened the wing window. A gush of cold air immediately struck their faces. Uncle, hands steady, raised his Nikon, whispering, "A little lower, Stewart. Ease in. Steady." The plane bounced and leveled to a hundred feet over a vineyard of Thompson grapes. The family had come out of their house. They were waving, all of them, waving hats and dish towels. Their dogs were leaping and barking.

Uncle shot a rapid succession of pictures and closed the plane window when they had passed the farm. He reloaded the Nikon. He turned to the boys, "Pretty exciting, *¿qué no?*"

Hector smiled with a set of chattering teeth. He was cold and miserable. A white-faced Mando mumbled, "Yeah, it's a lot of fun."

The plane banked sharply. Uncle once again opened the window and raised his camera. He aimed and the camera clicked *chew*, *chew*, *chew* as it shot frame after frame. Within a minute, he took twenty-four shots and among them, he figured, was one that would be perfect. The In-ouyes, Japanese-American farmers, would be proud.

As the plane banked west toward the airport,

Uncle spotted a vehicle on fire. He raised his Nikon and took a picture. He reloaded and fixed a zoom lens onto the camera. He told Stewart, "Lower us down, Stu. It looks like a UPS truck. I didn't know they went this far into the countryside."

"That ain't a UPS," Stewart disagreed. "It's an armored truck."

Hector said, "Looks like a tank to me."

"No, man," Mando answered, "it looks like Tío Lupe's old Chevy after he rolled it."

Uncle Julio said, "Quiet, you jokers. Something's happening down there. Looks serious."

Hector and Mando craned their necks to see. They saw a truck in the road, a puff of smoke rising. A car was parked next to it, and two men were hovering over the trunk.

While Stewart buzzed the truck, Uncle aimed the Nikon and took pictures. They buzzed a second time, and Uncle remarked, "Maybe I can sell it to the newspaper. I've been meaning to crack *The Fresno Bee*."

Stewart banked left and a choppy wind caught them as they gained altitude. They started back to the airport. Hector gripped his seat, which, he discovered, gave up a wad of cotton matting. Playfully, he tried to press the cotton into Mando's ear. Mando muttered, "That ain't gonna help if we crash."

But the plane leveled off and the flight home was uneventful. They descended smoothly. On landing, the plane crushed a tumbleweed that got caught under the landing gear. Stewart complained as the airplane taxied to the hangar. When business picked up, he promised, he would move his plane to the airport across town.

Hector was glad to get out of the plane. He jumped from the wing and felt his stomach rise to his throat. He felt giddy for a second, free and safe, and then uneasy when his uncle said, "We have another shoot."

"Another one?" Hector asked.

"*Simón.*"

"Do we have to get in this thing again?" Mando asked, pointing at the plane.

"No, we're going by car," Uncle Julio answered and started limping toward the parking lot with Hector and Mando in tow. He turned and waved to Stewart, "The check's in the mail."

"I hope so," Stewart hollered in the wind. "I gotta pay the gas bill by the fifteenth, or it's lights out."

They got into the car and drove across town. But this time, no matter how Uncle beat on the radio, the music wouldn't twang from the speakers. The country-western songs, it seemed, had clip-clopped to their trail's end.

They drove in silence to a canary-colored house.

"She's one of my best customers," Uncle Julio said as he got out of the car. He opened the trunk and brought out a heavy box that contained lights and tripods.

"Your best customer?" Hector asked.

"Mrs. Murguia pays in cash. No bounced checks to worry about. And she's a cute *vieja*."

Hector studied the house as he helped to carry the box to the front steps. There were rows of plastic roses pressed into the flower box. A tiny windmill turned on the front lawn. Twin flamingoes were stuck in the wet earth. Astroturf was glued to the front steps and a row of ceramic frogs dotted the steps. "It looks like a miniature golf course," he concluded.

"Yeah, it does," Mando agreed.

Uncle knocked and the door opened to the sounds of cats meowing.

"*Buenas tardes, señora,*" Uncle greeted respectfully.

"*Buenas tardes.*" She greeted him with a smile and her hands pressed to her heart. She was a woman in her seventies and wore a print dress of chickens and dogs. ¿"*Cómo se llaman sus niños?*" She pointed to Hector and Mando.

"This is my nephew Hector, and this is Mando, his friend."

"*Mucho gusto, señora*," the boys said with respect.

"*Pásen*," she instructed. She waved for them to come in, and the three wiped their feet carefully because they could see that her house was neat and orderly. When they entered, three orange cats jumped from the couch, their tails up in alarm. The cats were wearing pink bow ties.

Uncle put down his equipment. Hector and Mando did the same.

Two more cats came into the living room. They were gray and their bow ties were pink, too. They meowed, leaped playfully and rolled onto their backs.

"Open the box," Uncle said. "Take out the tall stand and medium reflector."

A striped cat sauntered into the room, his bow tie undone. He was licking his whiskers, having just eaten from a bowl of crunchies in the kitchen. His motor was purring deep in his chest.

"*Ay*, Fernando," Mrs. Murguia sighed softly. "You keep undoing your tie." She bent down with a grunt and, as she redid the bow tie, the cat licked her hands.

Uncle set up the camera on a tripod in the living room. He got a reading of the light. He adjusted the reflector and bounced the light off the ceiling. Then he took a Polaroid shot of Mrs.

Murguia holding the cat. "I'm ready," he finally said.

Mrs. Murguia gathered her cats — all ten, with a murky aquarium in the background — and cooed to them, "*Cálmesen*, you naughty *gatos*." The cats had started wrestling and chewing on each other's bow ties, boxing and throwing *pleitos*.

"Be cool," Uncle said to the cats as he redid one loose bow tie. Hector and Mando helped out.

"Mom wouldn't think they're cute," Hector said. He patted one cat and it pawed at him.

"These cats are better dressed than us, Hector," Mando said. "Heck, they could be goin' to the prom."

Once the cats settled around Mrs. Murguia, Uncle didn't waste time. He began to shoot. The Nikon *chew-chew-chewed* a succession of shots. And with each shot, the cats became more and more restless until they once again began to fight and rip their bow ties.

"Be cool," Uncle warned the cats. Hector and Mando redid the bow ties. Mrs. Murguia went into the kitchen to fetch a handful of cat nibbles.

"These *gatitos* are my best customers," Uncle said. "Every time Mrs. Murguia gets a new cat, she calls me up. She loves them more than anything."

Mrs. Murguia returned with a ladleful of cat nibbles that calmed them down. The cats were named Fernando, Cochino, Boots, Precioso, Rayo, Kitty, Little Kitty, Momma Kitty, Angel, and the new one was Novio Boy.

CHAPTER 3

A fter the photography shoot at Mrs. Murguia's, which was more of a chase around
the house after prancing cats with loose bow ties,
the three started back to the apartment. Uncle
pounded on the car radio with a clenched fist,
and once again a country-western song twanged
through the loudspeaker. When the song ended
there was a report of an armored-car robbery in
the area of Central Avenue. The drivers had been
bound and gagged, the newscaster reported, and
authorities said that fifty thousand dollars had
been stolen. The drivers could not describe the
robbers.

Hector looked up at his uncle, bright-eyed. He
swallowed and stuttered, "Unc, you thinking
what I'm thinking?"

Uncle looked at the boys. He pounded the
radio when country-western music started to
play again. The song ended as quickly as it had
started. "*Híjole*, I think we got something here."
He touched his chest, where his shirt pocket

25

drooped with three rolls of film. A scene of the robbery was in one of the rolls.

Uncle sped up, the windows of the Ford station wagon vibrating. He had thought of stopping for burgers and fries, but developing the film seemed more urgent than the hunger tying knots in their stomachs. When they arrived at the apartment, they skidded to a halt in the driveway, scaring two fat pigeons dunking their faces into a puddle.

The three unloaded the photography equipment. Without his cane, Uncle trotted to his mailbox and jumped for joy when he discovered a check that had been owed him for two months. He tore open the letter; a check for $79.59 stared at him.

"I thought your leg was hurt?" Hector asked.

"Running for money doesn't give me any pain," Uncle answered. He folded the check and slipped it into his wallet. "We eat out tonight. But let's develop these first." He took the rolls of film from his shirt pocket and juggled them as he limped up the steps to the apartment.

Uncle checked his answering machine with the hope that there might be more business. He played it back and heard a woman yelling, "Is Rick there? I wanna talk to Rick!"

Uncle's face spread with a smirk. He pressed the erase button and said to Hector and Mando,

"The *ruca's* got the wrong number. Let's develop the film. Remember, once we close the door, you guys can't open it. It'll ruin the film."

The three huddled together in the bathroom, a makeshift darkroom with a red light over the mirror. After developing the negatives, Uncle shot the images onto photographic paper. He placed the paper into a pan filled with a chemical solution and, whistling through his mustache as he worked, swished the pan back and forth. Slowly images appeared on the paper.

"Hey, Mando, it's you and me at the train station," Hector said with happy surprise.

"Yeah, we look cool," Mando said. "Hey, wait a minute, it looks like my eyes are closed."

Hector looked closely. "Yeah, but I can see some *laganas* in their corners."

"No way, *ese*. *Chále*," Mando responded, pushing his friend playfully.

Other images began to appear, images mostly of the Inouye farm. But the third roll held pictures of the armored car. Uncle rocked the pan, cooing, "Man, I can get a job with the *The Fresno Bee*. Maybe win the Pulitzer Prize for photo journalism. Be a famous Chicano photographer!"

Uncle was giddy with excitement. With wooden tongs, he raised the pictures out of the solution. He shook them lightly, a sprinkle of solution splattering to the floor. He held them up to the red light, one eye squinting. "Yeah, we even got a license plate number on that car — XJIP30."

"Let me see, Unc," Hector begged. He took the pictures and examined the images. He saw two men bending over a trunk of a car — one fat guy and one guy skinny as a hoe. He was excited. He felt that if he could solve a crime, especially one involving big money, he could return by jet, not train, to East Los. He could return with his pockets brimming with dollar bills.

"This is *bad*." Hector smiled dreamily as he handed the images to Mando.

The three gave themselves high-fives and left the bathroom. Uncle said he would make larger prints after lunch. They washed up and ate their Super Bowl salad, grinning over their discovery.

"You think you should call the police?" Hector asked. His cheek was fat with olives. The tip of his fork was red with a speared cherry. "The salad's pretty good."

"*Simón*," Mando agreed. He speared two cherries with one thrust.

"Yeah, we'll call them in time. I'm gonna call the newspaper first," Uncle said. He balanced a forkful of peas — the spectators — and shoveled it into his mouth. He chewed thoughtfully as he looked at his small apartment, where the furniture was all brown. He got up from the table and called directory assistance for the number to *The Fresno Bee*.

"City desk at the *Bee*," Uncle asked with a pencil in his hand. He looked up from the telephone, his hand over the mouthpiece. "Eat your peas, *escuincles*."

Hector and Mando shoveled peas into their mouths and had to agree that they tasted better than the peas they got at home.

When Uncle got the number he immediately called the city desk.

"Julio Silva," he said. "You know that robbery on Central. Well, I got a hot tip. . . ."

Uncle started from the beginning. He explained that he'd gotten a job shooting the Inouye farm in Parlier. He explained that they were flying a Cessna 143 and that he had brought his nephew and his nephew's friend along for the ride. He explained that they first thought the armored car was a UPS delivery van. He explained how they flew two times over the scene of the robbery, and was starting to explain how he and Stewart had met on a "thirty and over" softball team when a voice on the other end screamed, "All right already. Get down here. Show me those negatives!"

Uncle held his hand over the mouthpiece. He said to the boys, "I got the *vato*'s attention. You have to just lay it on thick when you talk to the Man."

Uncle scribbled down a name — Clarence T. Wearwell. He hung up and told the boys, "It's half time. Leave the salad for later."

They left the apartment and drove across town. Uncle was happy and excited, but every time he saw a car like the robbers' car, a blue Caprice, he shuddered. At a red light, he got nervous when a Caprice pulled up next to them. But when he craned his neck to look over, he saw that the driver was an older woman wearing navy blue gloves. She looked like she was off to church. A bud of red lipstick darkened her mouth.

They squeezed into a narrow parking space at *The Fresno Bee* building. As they climbed out of the car, Uncle touched his shirt pocket. "Here goes," Uncle said, as he led the boys inside the gray building to the reception desk. A security guard led them to a conference room, where Hector and Mando helped themselves to bottled water in little paper cups. The water was so cold it almost hurt when it flowed down their throats.

A man in a rumpled suit came into the room. He held out a meaty hand and said, "Clarence T. Wearwell."

"Julio Silva," Uncle said. "These are my boys."

Clarence T. Wearwell nodded at Hector and Mando, and then turned his attention to Julio. "Have a seat. Let me see what you have."

The four of them sat down. Uncle brought out the negatives and gave them to Wearwell, who held them up to the overhead light, one eye winking as he studied the images. He took his eyeglasses from his shirt pocket, breathed on the lenses, wiped them, and put them on. He studied the negatives a second time. "Hmmmm," he said finally as he stroked his chin. He handed them back to Uncle. "Seems like you have plenty of evidence here, even the license plate. We could use this." He thought deeply and then looked at Hector and Mando. "But first, have you boys ever been interviewed?"

"Us?" the boys nearly shouted as they suddenly became big-eyed with excitement.

"Well, the police interrogated me once," Mando admitted. He gazed down at the floor and muttered, "My stupid brother wrote his name in wet cement, and he blamed me. The *tonto*! It wasn't even my name!"

"This is different. We have a column called 'Today's Youth,'" Wearwell said cheerfully. "We have a reporter who'll interview you about your little escapade. What school do you go to?"

"We're from East Los," Hector answered. "We're seventh-graders at Virgil Junior High."

"This is even better. Kids from the big city." He unhooked his walkie-talkie from his belt and called, "Ms. Moreno, please come to conference room B." He then looked at Uncle, his thumb tapping the end of the table. "If you don't mind, can we make prints of these?"

"Well, yeah, but I was thinking — " Uncle started to say.

"Of course, we'll pay you for your services. Three hundred about right?"

"Sounds good," Uncle said, gulping at the figure. He began to wonder if he had to share the sum with Stewart. He decided he would.

When Ms. Vicky Moreno came into the room, Uncle stood up with a smile, dazzled. Ms. Moreno was tall, slender, and with a slight overbite that made Uncle touch his throat. He thought she was beautiful. Her eyes were clear and her mouth was pink as the inside of a rose.

"Vicky, I wish you would interview these two boys," Wearwell instructed. He rose from his seat and muttered into his walkie-talkie, "I want a rush in the lab. I need some prints immediately."

Vicky smiled at Hector and Mando. "We'll find out first who they are."

"I'm Hector Beltran," Hector said.

"I'm Armando Tafolla the first," Mando said.

"What do you mean the 'the first'?" Hector asked his friend.

"I mean I'm the one and only."

"I know a guy in San José who has the same name. It's real common, dude."

"He's the second, I'm the first," Mando argued, jabbing a finger at Hector's chest.

Uncle butted in and said, "And I'm the uncle of these two sweet knuckleheads. My name's Julio Silva." He offered his hand to the woman reporter, who shook it lightly, a cool smile starting at the corner of her mouth.

"Mr. Silva, I would like you to come with me," Wearwell said. He looked up at the clock that read two-thirty. "I have a meeting at three o'clock, so why don't we move on?"

"Can't I stay here?" Uncle asked with the painful look of a scolded dog. "Maybe I can help?"

"Vicky can handle the interview. I think it's best that we get these negatives developed. If we have time, I'll show you around."

Wearwell started to lead a reluctant Uncle from the room by the elbow, but he pulled away and whispered in Hector's ear. "Listen, Hector, I want you as cleverly as you can to tell Ms. Moreno that I think she's sweet-looking. Can you do that? Can you tell her I'm an all right uncle?"

Hector looked up and said, "Vicky, I think my uncle likes you."

"*Cállate*," Uncle scolded playfully. He smiled at Vicky. "The boy has an uncontrollable mouth. And sensitive ears." He pulled on Hector's ear, and left with Wearwell.

After they left the room, Vicky asked the boys to sit down. The interview began with questions about family, friends, hobbies, pets, favorite food, and movies, and finally aspirations.

"Well, I'd like a little of the reward money," Hector said after much thought.

"What reward money?" Vicky asked.

"Didn't the guy tell you?" Mando asked.

"You mean Mr. Wearwell? No."

"We saw this robbery," Hector began to explain. "I was at the controls of the airplane when I told my uncle, 'Hey, *ese*, there is trouble down below.' " Hector gave a mean look at Mando, as if to say, "Don't rock my story."

Vicky was busy writing in her pad.

"Yeah, that's right," Mando agreed. "Hector was at the controls because I was tired of driving the plane."

Hector shot a stern look at Mando but didn't say anything to ruffle his version of the story. Mando continued: "Yeah, Uncle Julio was — "

"Julio is your uncle?" Ms. Moreno asked.

"*My* uncle," Hector said, pointing a finger at

his chest. "I'll explain it all. I'm better at words than Mando. You see, I was flying the plane and I saw some heavy *chingadasos* on the ground and lowered the plane so that my uncle could take some pictures."

"Yeah, I had to help Hector's *tío* aim the camera," Mando interrupted, "because he didn't get too much sleep because this woman kept calling him and asking for Rick."

Hector gave Mando another mean look. "What are you talkin' about?"

"What are *you* talkin' about?"

"I asked you first."

"I asked second."

"Boys! Hector, Mando! Let's not argue," Vicky scolded lightly. She shook her pad and then said, "I need your help and cooperation. I heard about the robbery. Can you tell me exactly what you saw?"

Hector and Mando leveled with Vicky. Hector even said that they were scared of flying, that neither of them helped fly the plane or take the picture. They said they mostly wished that they had stayed on the ground because it was cold and the plane had rust holes that scared them to death. Mando said that he was scared that his foot would punch through one of the holes and that he would be sucked out of the plane and that his body would end up splattered in a cow field. He said that he would rather be killed by Bertha Sanchez than fall from an airplane.

"Really?" Hector asked with surprise. "I would rather get killed in a plane crash. Bertha hits too hard."

Hector went on to describe the armored car and the blue Chevy Caprice license plate number XJIP30. He told Vicky that there were two men, both in greenish jackets. One was as thick as an oil barrel, and maybe just as greasy. He explained it all without a touch of fantasy, and then, with a sigh and nod of his head, confessed, "I think my uncle likes you. And that's the truth."

Vicky smiled from embarrassment. "That's nice to hear. Now let's get a picture of the two of you."

CHAPTER 4

Freddie Bork, a portly man with his left pinkie finger cut to the knuckle, rattled the newspaper and yelled, "Huey, get out of the bathroom. We're in trouble! Two little punks from L.A. squealed on us!"

Freddie Bork and Huey "Crybaby" Walker were the thugs who had robbed the armored car and tied the drivers into knots. Huey had cried over the roughhousing, but later felt pretty happy when he held bundled packets of hundred-dollar bills, all clean and smelling sweet. With tears on his eyelashes he slapped his wrist with a package of bills and joked, "Bad boy!"

Huey came out of the bathroom, his face stinging from after-shave lotion called Brisky Day. His face was nicked where his razor had glided recklessly over a hairy mole. His eyes were small and red as the crayon scribblings of a mad child. He looked scared, worried, dark with suspicion. He snatched the newspaper from Freddie Bork and read the news, his purplish lips moving over each word. Huey read about the airplane that had taken pictures of the heist, and read about a photographer with a Nikon and a zoom lens. He read about kids named Hector and Armando and the A average they maintained at Virgil Junior High in East Los Angeles. As he reached the end of the article, true to his name, he started to cry.

"Crying won't get you nowhere," said Freddie, the brains behind the heist and the muscle when things got rough. His face was dark with anger. He snapped a wooden match between his thumb and index finger and sneered, "I hate it when kids try to be do-gooders." He hated most kids. He thought they got too much of the world, and he should know. He had been married five times and had fathered five children, each with demands for sweets and love.

Freddie lifted the newspaper and studied the faces of Hector and Mando, both smiling from ear to ear. He took a slurp of his coffee, which was barely warm. "They're lying," he muttered between his teeth. "They don't look like A students to me."

"What are we gonna do?" Huey asked from across the kitchen table where they sat. He was staring at the floor, popping the knuckles on his huge fists.

"We'll get rid of the car first," Freddie said.

"But I like that car," Huey said.

"What do you want, a nice car or a prison cell?"

Huey sighed but didn't say anything. A few of his tears fell like rain on the thin, fuzzy carpet.

"Then we'll take care of those two punks!" Freddie snarled. He massaged the nub of his pinkie, which throbbed whenever he was upset. "Huey, quit your cryin' and get me some coffee — black!" He was feeling irritable. He got up with a groan and, kicking off his shoes, sat on the bed of their motel room. He took out a pair of nail clippers and began paring his fingernails. He pared them and then filed them, whistling as he worked.

"Those punks. I got four punks of my own," Freddie said.

"I thought you had five punks," Huey said as he brought them both cups of coffee.

"One doesn't like me, so I don't count him."

Huey took a sip of coffee. "That's a shame, your own kid not liking you. Shows no respect." He took another sip of coffee and remarked, "Freddie, you're good people. The best."

"I try to be," Freddie said, touched by the compliment.

They clinked mugs to that, and turned on the motel television to kill time.

CHAPTER 5

Hector and Mando huddled together as they read the morning edition of *The Fresno Bee*. They were glowing and reading the "Today's Youth" column for the fourth time. They read the inch-long paragraphs and had to agree that in the picture they looked handsome, standing nearly cheek to cheek and smiling for the camera.

"But we're not A-average students," Mando said. "I get mostly C's." Mando's best subject was homeroom, but that didn't count for much when grades were handed out.

"Yeah, maybe we're not great students," Hector agreed, "but you know we're pretty smart." He had accumulated a row of C's and B's year after year with a sprinkling of A's, mostly in P.E. But his attendance was solid. He was sent off each day in an ironed shirt, his mother on the porch shouting, "You better behave yourself."

Mando thought for a moment. He never considered himself dumb, just lazy. Also, there were too many brothers and sisters in his house. Three shared his bedroom that looked out onto the bar Under the Skies of Vera Cruz. "Yeah, maybe it's our environment," Mando said, echoing an article that he had read in the newspaper about why children do poorly in school.

"Yeah, we ain't dummies."

Uncle came out of the bedroom, rubbing his fists over his sleepy eyes. He yawned and asked, "What time is it?"

"Uncle we got a surprise," Hector said. "Remember when we were at the newspaper office yesterday?"

"Yeah, what about it?" He retied his robe and staggered to the kitchen to put water on to boil for coffee.

"We were interviewed by the lady you like."

Uncle's interest perked up. Suddenly he wasn't sleepy one bit. "Did you get her telephone number?"

"Whose number?" Hector said innocently.

"Don't be a *tonto*. You know who," Uncle said.

Uncle had been pestering the boys since the day before about Ms. Moreno. But Hector and Mando remained quiet about their interview in order to surprise Uncle. They wanted him to find out about the "Today's Youth" column while he was grubbing on a plate of *huevos con chorizo*. No matter how much he grilled them, no matter

41

how much he promised to buy them any CD's they wanted, they wouldn't crack. They kept saying, "Chill out, Unc, you'll see tomorrow."

Tomorrow arrived and the newspaper arrived, hurled on the wet grass by some guy on a motor scooter. Hector and Mando were in the public's eyes, including Freddie Bork and Huey "Cry-baby" Walker.

"No, we didn't get her telephone number. We're in her column 'Today's Youth.' Here, look at it."

"You're in *what*?" He took the folded newspaper from Hector and shook it open.

" 'Today's Youth,' " Mando said. "That's a funny phrase. It should be 'Today's *Vato Loco*.' "

Uncle leaned against the kitchen counter and read the column, his lips moving over each word. When he finished, he scowled at the boys. "They published this?"

"It's cool, huh?" Hector asked proudly.

"No, it's *not* cool."

"It's not?"

Uncle rubbed his chin and returned to the kitchen when the kettle began to whistle and rattle. "No! It means that we're a target."

"A target?" Hector asked.

"You shouldn't have said anything! Those thugs might come after us."

"But there's an article on the front page, too,"

Hector said as he followed his uncle into the kitchen. Uncle took the newspaper from Hector, read about the armed robbery and almost jumped when he saw Hector, Mando, and himself named as eyewitnesses. Stewart was also mentioned, but only his first name.

"Hector, Mando!" he said as he slapped the newspaper. He looked vaguely around the room. "We're in trouble. These guys are probably gonna come after us."

Hector and Mando looked at each other. They hadn't thought about the robbers. They had completely forgotten about them as they blabbed to the reporter. They were eager to get their faces and names in the newspaper — but they weren't thinking of the obituary page.

When the telephone started to ring, the three of them jumped. They looked at each other, too frightened to answer it. They walked over and stared at the telephone.

"Should we get it?" Hector asked.

"No, just let it ring," Uncle answered.

What if it's the robbers? Hector wondered. He was suddenly sorry for blabbing to Ms. Moreno, but she'd seemed so nice. She had even given them each a ten-dollar food certificate for the McDonald's on Shaw Avenue.

The phone rang four times before the answering machine kicked in. After Uncle Julio's curt recorded message, a woman's voice demanded, "Is Rick there? I wanna talk to Rick!"

Uncle laughed and said, "It's Rick's ole' girlfriend. He got out of town when she started to get *loca*. You'll understand one day."

Uncle fixed himself instant coffee and told the boys to help themselves to cold cereal. Hector and Mando had already eaten, but if they hadn't, they would have been too depressed to shove spoonfuls of Captain Crunch into their big mouths.

Uncle took his coffee to the couch. He asked, "So what's Ms. Moreno's first name?"

"Vicky," Hector said. "I had a girlfriend named Vicky. But she spelled her name with an 'i' not a 'y.' "

"Nah, you never had a girlfriend," Uncle said, getting comfortable on the couch.

"I did, too," Hector said and turned to Mando. "Huh, Mando."

"Don't remember."

"You do too, man."

"But what was *my* Vicky like?" Uncle asked, interrupting their argument. He blew on his coffee, took a sip, and waited to hear about her.

"She's pretty nice, but she tricked us. She said she wanted to hear about us and the robbery," Hector said.

"Did she say she was married?"

"No."

"Did she say if she were going out with a dude?"

"No."

"Did she tell you where she lived?"

"No."

"Did she tell you *anything*?"

"No, we're the ones who did all the telling." Hector wasn't feeling too good about blabbering. He asked his uncle if he and Mando could take a walk around the block.

"Okay, but don't go far," Uncle warned them. "I don't want you two to get hurt. Your mom would kill me, Hector." He took a sip of his coffee and said, "Vicky. That's a nice name. Common sense name."

Hector and Mando left the apartment, the collars of their jackets up like sails. The day was cold and the morning sun hung in the east behind a feathery fog. The trees hung with dew. The lawns were icy and carved up with bicycle tracks. They walked up the street in silence, their breath before them, white as a fistful of dirty cotton. They turned the corner and began to walk up a business street.

"Mando, when you get big, where would you like to live?" Hector asked.

"I wanna live near water. Maybe Hawaii." They walked in silence, almost two blocks before Mando asked, "How 'bout you?"

"The moon," Hector joked. "It's safer up there."

They stopped in front of a Denny's Restaurant, where a row of newspaper racks stood. They stared at the front page of the newspaper. The headline screamed at them: ARMORED CAR ROBBERY. The smaller headline said EYE-WITNESSES' REPORT.

"Yeah, Uncle Julio's right, Mando. We're probably in big trouble," Hector moaned. The last time they were in serious trouble was when they locked themselves out of Mando's house and tried to get in by sliding down the chimney. But Mando got stuck. When the police and fire trucks arrived, gumballs flashing, they pulled him out and took the boys to a correctional center, where they were booked for breaking and entering.

That was two years ago. Now they were in Fresno, with their faces splashed on thousands of newspapers. Hector jumped at every honking horn or tire screech. It seemed to him that every car on the road was a blue Caprice with two thugs fondling handguns in their pockets.

CHAPTER
6

Freddie Bork and Huey "Crybaby" Walker got out of their blue Chevy Caprice, the keys still in the ignition. Huey was sad about their plan for leaving the car for someone else to steal. He had stolen it from a pastor in Idaho, that and the pastor's wallet and leatherbound Bible, and he was awfully sorry to give up such a fine-running vehicle. He felt like crying, but he knew it would just make Freddie mad. He blew the car a Hollywood kiss and caught up with Freddie, who was hiking up his pants. They were going to get breakfast at a Denny's Restaurant. They took a booth near the window so they could see who would steal the car. The windows were rolled down, the door slightly ajar.

The waitress approached with pad in hand, pencil wagging between her chubby fingers.

"I'll take the Wake Me Up," Freddie said, not even looking at the menu. "Tomato juice as well."

Huey pointed at the picture he wanted, the

picture of waffles and three sausages all in a neat row. "I want that. And coffee."

"Just our luck," Freddie lamented after the waitress had gone. "An airplane passing by, and some jerk with a camera. How do you like that?"

"I don't see the problem," Huey said. "We got the money."

"You don't see the problem? You don't see nothing," Freddie muttered, voice edged with anger. "The problem is that every time we rob someone, we make more problems for ourselves. Remember that guy in Tulare?"

They had robbed a biker in the washroom of a bar called Honey-Dew-Drop-Inn. But the biker with no front teeth wouldn't go down no matter how many times they punched him. The biker clawed and punched back and managed to yell for his other biker friends. They were barely able to escape from the bar, and when they did, a herd of bikers chased Freddie and Huey clear out of the valley into Nevada. They were driving a Toyota then, one with no guts and plenty of blue smoke. If the bikers hadn't run out of gas, they would have been meat for the wolves and bones for tumbleweeds to catch on.

"Oh yeah, them," Huey said. He shivered at the memory. All they had gotten from the biker was a pair of nail clippers and the scare of their lives.

"It's just bad luck," Freddie said. He lifted his eyes when the waitress brought coffee but didn't thank her. He shook a packet of sugar into his coffee and laced it with a splash of milk. "We're gonna have to teach those kids, and the uncle, too."

"I hate the thought of hurting kids," Huey said, his eyes starting to mist. He sipped his coffee and looked out the window. A man with a shopping cart was circling the Caprice. He stopped his cart, opened the car door, and started rifling through the glove compartment.

"Well, maybe we can toss them in the river," Freddie suggested. "That'll scare them."

"But what if they can't swim?"

"All kids can swim."

Their breakfast came, a factory of steam rising from the waffles and eggs. Freddie looked up but didn't thank the waitress.

"Hey, look," Huey said, pointing with his knife stuck with a pat of butter.

Outside, a man and a woman were arguing over who was going to steal the car. They were pushing each other, and through the plate glass at Denny's Freddie and Huey made out the words, "I saw it first!"

"I hate that!" said Freddie. "The woman should let the guy have the car. The dude saw it first! Crimeney, no one's civil anymore." He poked the yellow of his eggs and watched it run like lava into a pile of hash browns. He held up his coffee cup. "Waitress!"

"The waffles are the best," Huey said, face close to the plate. A sloppery syrup filled the small squares of the waffles. The sausages were slightly curled, almost like canoes.

Outside, the car started. Both the man and woman were in it, an agreement apparently having been reached. The engine revved, and the blue Chevy Caprice, Huey's favorite stolen car of all time, pulled out of the parking lot with its own set of problems, mechanical and otherwise.

CHAPTER 7

Hector and Mando had returned from their walk shivering from the damp air. Uncle was dressed and sitting at the kitchen table, balancing his checkbook. A stack of bills stood tall on the table.

"Hey, you guys," he greeted them without looking up as the boys stamped their feet on a rug. He paused for a second and then, scooting his chair around, said, "Don't worry. Nothin's going to happen to us."

While they were on their walk, he figured he had been hard on them. If he were a kid and a newspaper reporter said, "I'm going to put you in tomorrow's news," he would have blabbed everything about his life, including the time he stole two bicycles, both from his cousin Lupe.

"We're not worried," Hector lied as he huddled over the floor furnace, warming himself.

"Yeah, we throw some *chingadasos* if they mess with us," Mando said. "Sock them in the jaw if they fool with these homeboys."

"That's the way to think," Uncle said with irony. Right there, at the kitchen table, he concluded that the younger generation had seen too many Stallone and Schwarzenegger movies. He got up from the chair. "We're gonna drive down to Parlier and deliver the pictures to the Inouyes."

Right after meeting with Wearwell, Uncle had taken the negatives to Paul Kanzaki's Photo Studio. He had asked Paul to make prints and touch them up with color. He had an appointment to pick up the prints at nine-thirty.

The boys jumped when the telephone rang. Uncle limped over to the telephone and answered it. "Hello," he said.

It was Vicky on the other end.

"Well, hello, Vicky," Uncle said as cheerfully as he could. "No, no, we're awake. We get up early. Did we see the paper? Oh, sure we did. The boys were happy to be written up."

But Vicky wasn't so happy. She called to apologize for the story's publication. It wasn't supposed to appear for another week, or until after the robbers were apprehended and locked away. She was sorry that it had run without notice, an error by her assistant.

"I'm sorry that you're sorry," Uncle said in a suave voice. He leaned against the wall and with his finger twirled the cord. "If it will make you feel better, why don't you have dinner with me and my boys?"

Hector jumped away from the heater, which had gotten too hot for comfort. He shook his head at Uncle. He felt his uncle was being silly for a grown man, hitting on a woman he'd only known for five minutes.

A smile lit Uncle's face. The answer was *yes*. He hung up the telephone and rubbed his hands together. "We're goin' out, *hombres*. What do you wanna have, chicken or pizza?"

"Pizza," the boys screamed.

Uncle paused for a second and thought. "On second thought, we'll have Thai food. No, we'll let Vicky choose." He clapped his hands and said, "Come on, *ándale*. We have to get the pictures delivered."

They drove down to Paul Kanzaki's Photo Studio, which was located on the west side of Fresno, the bad side of town. Two bums were drinking from a bottle when they parked the car in front of the studio. A dog with mismatched eyes was sniffing a burger wrapper.

They got out of the car and said "Good morning" to the bums and entered Paul's studio. Paul was in the back, touching up the Inouye family farm with a little color — green on the orange trees and lawns, and pink and blue for the sky. He used a nice brown for the muddy tractor path.

"Paul!" Uncle yelled.

Paul, a Japanese-American himself, came out from the back with his smock untied. He proudly held up the photograph. He asked, "What do you think, Julio?"

Uncle grinned and applauded, "The Picasso of farm pictures. Paul, I don't know how you do it."

"With pastels and a steady hand," Paul said. He then added that he had once dated Tad Inouye's wife, back in high school. They were sweethearts for three weeks, and then just friends for the rest of his life.

"Is that right?" Uncle said with surprise.

"Yeah, but she married that farmer. Her hands are probably all rough."

"Too bad for her."

"Yeah, she could have had me, and all this." He gestured at what hung on the walls: photographs that were yellowed, dusty, and curled in their frames. He looked at Hector and Mando and asked, "Are you his assistants?"

"Yeah," Hector said. "I'm also his nephew."

"I'm Mando," said Mando.

"They're visiting me from East Los Angeles.

Did you read about them in the newspaper?"

Paul shook his head no. He usually read his newspaper in the afternoon.

"We're in 'Today's Youth,' " Hector said.

Paul's eyes sparkled but he didn't say anything. He then looked up at Julio and said, "That's forty-three dollars, Julio."

Julio wrote out a check.

"Okay, Paul, but can you cash it after two o'clock? That's when I'm doing the banking," Uncle said. He showed Paul, a softy at heart, the check from *The Fresno Bee* for three hundred dollars. That would go into his checking account along with the Inouye check.

"Okay," he said. "Say hi to Kimiko for me."

"Who's Kimiko?"

"Inouye's wife. My ole' sweetheart."

Uncle and the boys left Paul's studio, closing the door gently behind them. Uncle said "Have a good day" to the bums, who raised their wine bottles in salute, returning the greeting. Julio opened the back of his Ford station wagon and fumbled through a cardboard box. He brought out a picture frame. He dusted it off with his sleeve, fogged the glass with his breath, and wiped it clean before he fit the picture of the Inouye farm into the frame.

They then got into the car and drove to the

freeway, Uncle still feeling happy because he had a job nearly finished and a date with a news reporter.

"Do we have to have Thai food?" Hector asked. "Why can't we have American food, like pizza?"

"It's up to Vicky. She's our guest," Uncle answered. "Maybe Vicky will want to go to Di-Cicco's, order the works." Uncle was in much too good a mood to argue.

Hector gave Mando the thumbs-up sign and then fell silent as he watched the roadside become a patch of farms—vineyards and orchards that, in season, grew grapes, plums, nectarines, almonds, all the fruits of the world in one long valley. He watched a tractor cut across a muddy field, a plume of smoke rising from its steel exhaust. He watched children laughing and beating each other with plastic bats, and huge blackbirds sitting on a barbed wire fence, beaks open and swallowing the wind of rushing traffic. He watched the valley pass, acre after brown acre.

They pulled into Parlier, a small town with one traffic light. They got themselves sodas, and then drove outside of town, east to where the Inouye farm lay.

"Drink up quick," Uncle said. His cold soda was propped between his legs.

Hector drank so fast that he burned his nostrils. He asked his uncle, "What do the Inouyes grow?"

"Nectarines, I think," Uncle said. "Some oranges."

They drove along a country road for two miles. On each side of the road stood orange trees.

"Here we are," Uncle said. He recognized the farm from the white fence and the tall palm tree.

As they pulled into the driveway that led to the house, Hector noticed a parked car. He got onto his knees and looked back. Two men were sitting in the car, not moving.

Uncle pulled into the driveway and honked his horn. Two German shepherds came out of the rain-warped house, barking.

"These dogs are scary," Hector said.

"Looks like they want some Mexican food," Mando said, referring to his legs.

"They're tame. Nothin' to worry about." Uncle climbed out of the car, cooing, "Nice doggie. Hey, be cool!" One of the dogs had raised his front legs onto Uncle's chest. The dog was as tall as Uncle.

Mr. Inouye, followed by his wife who was slipping into a sweater, came out of the house yelling for his dogs to shut up. He picked up an orange that was on the ground and tossed it.

The dogs, tongues wagging, went chasing after the orange.

"So what do you have, Mr. Silva? Let's see," Mr. Inouye asked. He took the framed picture from Uncle. He held it up for his wife to see. Their faces glowed with pride as they admired their farm, all eighty acres. "Look, you can see me," Mr. Inouye remarked. He tapped the glass with a work-worn finger. He was on his tractor. "Looks real fine, Mr. Silva. Real fine."

The dogs returned with orange pulp between their teeth. Hector picked up another orange and hurled it. The dogs went racing after it.

Uncle took a batch of other photographs, ones that were not colored, all 8 × 10's, from a folder. "These are yours for the same price, too." Mrs. Inouye took them from Uncle, who noticed that her hands were soft, not rough, long and white, not stubby from pulling fruit from the branches. He realized that she was still attractive, beautiful even. He wouldn't have the heart to tell Paul that she was still stunning after all these years.

They did their business standing in the muddy driveway, Hector and Mando taking turns playing fetch with the dogs whose teeth were piling up with orange pulp.

"Are these your sons, Julio?" Mrs. Inouye asked.

"Yeah, in a way. These are my boys for the weekend," Uncle said.

"It's nice to meet you," Mrs. Inouye said. Her cheeks were red from the cold. Her hair was slightly mussed from the wind.

"You have a nice farm," Hector said.

"Pretty big," Mando said. "And nice dogs." For the tenth time, Mando tossed another orange and the dogs took off, tails wagging.

They concluded their deal, which included a bag of oranges for the boys, and waved good-bye. The three climbed back into the car. Hector waved to the dogs, who seemed sad that they were leaving. The dogs then started barking and ran after them as they rolled slowly down the driveway. Hector thought of tossing the dogs another orange, but he didn't want to waste one of his own. He tore into an orange, and Mando tore into one that was big as a softball.

When they pulled out of the farm, Hector spied the parked car. He nudged Mando's shoulder and said, "Check it out, man." Mando stopped chewing. He got onto his knees and looked over the seat at the car that was dark and spooky and flecked with mud the color of dry blood.

CHAPTER 8

After they left Denny's Restaurant, hiking up their pants and sucking on toothpicks, Freddie and Huey wandered down the street. They stopped in front of a used car dealer. A guy in rubber boots was washing cars, getting them ready for the day, which was gray and cold. Freddie hoped that the keys might still be in some of the ignitions. He hoped that the worker was not too bright.

"What kinda car you want?" Freddie asked, eyeing a row of late model American cars.

"How 'bout a Buick? We haven't driven one in a long time. Since we were in Bakersfield," Huey said.

When the telephone rang, the worker dropped the hose on the ground, where it continued to spray. He hustled over to the office, a trailer with colorful plastic flags.

"What a waste of water," Freddie sighed. "It's a cryin' shame. Huey, check out that Buick *there.*" Freddie pointed to a late-model red Buick Regal.

Huey slunk over and saw the keys on the seat. He opened the door, got in, and motioned to Freddie saying, "It's even got electric seats."

Freddie hurried over. He got in and peeked at the trailer. The worker was still on the telephone, a donut in his hand.

"Ease it out. Let's go," said Freddie as he adjusted his power seat. He opened the glove compartment and saw that, except for a handful of paper clips, it was empty.

Huey jumped the curb and sped away, not even glancing into the rearview mirror. They raced toward Chandler air field.

Earlier, at breakfast, as they sliced through waffles and sausages and poked the hearts out of their eggs, they had discussed where the photographer's plane could have taken off and landed. They narrowed it to Chandler air field, where small planes were kept, mostly biplane crop dusters. They drove to the airport, feeling good. The Buick had a smooth ride and plenty of visibility.

"It's a nice car," Huey said. "American cars are gettin' better."

"Yeah, it's smooth," Freddie said, closing his eyes and slumping down as if he were in a bathtub. He was feeling lazy from his breakfast.

At the airport, they parked the car in the handicapped zone and didn't even bother to limp into the pinkish-colored building. Although there was no one there in the foyer, they could hear the echo of talk in a far office.

Freddie walked over to a drinking fountain that was spurting water. He stepped on the pedal and the water stopped. "I hate it when people waste water," he complained. He turned and looked around, letting out a burp from his heavy breakfast. There were pictures of airplanes on all the walls, and photographs of aviators with thin mustaches. They were taken long ago, and Freddie assumed that they were all dead and buried.

"Let's check the board," Freddie suggested, hooking his thumb at the bulletin board in the hallway. He hoped maybe the photographer kept a business card tacked to the board. Most of what hung on the bulletin board were ads for airplanes for sale. Freddie, though, had to laugh when he came across a handwritten ad that read, "I listen." He tore it down and showed Huey. "Look at this crazy stuff. The guy listens and wants to get paid for it. Crazy people."

Stewart came in, wrench in hand and grease all the way to his elbows.

Freddie turned and said, "Good morning," friendly-like. He wet his lips and asked, "You know a photographer, one who works from the sky?"

Stewart paused and then said, "Sure. Actually, it's me and my friend Julio Silva."

Freddie became bright with interest. "Yeah, we're looking to do a little aerial photography. *Pronto*."

Huey gave Stewart a big smile.

"We'd be pleased to help out," Stewart said. "A farm or factory?"

"Both. You have the number of your friend?"

Stewart didn't have to look through his address book for Julio's telephone number. He put his wrench down on the table in the hallway and wrote Julio's number and address on a piece of paper. He handed it to Freddie. "Give us a call. The fog's been bad, but usually around three o'clock the weather is pretty good."

"You done a recent job?" Freddie asked. "We'll need references."

"The Inouye farm in Parlier just yesterday," Stewart said and wrote down the address of the farm. "You can get a reference from them. In fact, Julio's delivering the photograph this morning."

Freddie liked this. He had the photographer's

telephone number and a place to find him. He thanked Stewart and left the building with Huey leading the way.

Although he had read the article about their robbery a dozen times, Freddie bought another newspaper, a fresh one, from the rack outside the building. They got in their Buick and Freddie read while they pulled out of the driveway and drove toward the freeway.

"See what I tole' you?" Freddie said with a grin on his face. "The armored car drivers are keeping their mouths shut. They won't talk. They know better." He took out the cigarette-lighter pistol on his waist. When he pulled the trigger, a small flame shot out of the barrel. He blew the flame out and put the lighter back in his holster.

"I felt sorry for those drivers. They both seemed like family men," Huey said, suddenly sad. "It almost made me cry."

"They're probably divorced or mean to their wives and kids. Anyways, crying's not good for you. It'll make your face wrinkled." Freddie turned the page and saw a large ad for wholesale meats. "Great prices. Two twenty-nine a pound for sirloin."

Huey glanced over at the newspaper and nodded his head. "Good deal."

They got off the freeway at Manning and drove

east. Within ten miles, they were in Parlier. At a convenience store they got directions from a mother with two babies in her arms and two others poking around the candy rack. Huey bought the kids candy and tickled under their chins.

"You're a softy," Freddie said as they returned to the car. "It's not good for you."

They drove to the Inouye farm and parked the Buick on the side of the road. It was all country, quiet and cold. Huey got out and plucked three oranges from a tree. He returned to the car, a chill running down his back. They used a Swiss army knife to open the oranges and a wad of restaurant napkins to wipe away the juice on their fingers.

"But what if they don't come?" Huey asked.

"We'll eat oranges, then," Freddie said. He looked around. The fog was thick between the branches of the trees, almost spooky. A cat was sniffing a crushed cardboard box. Freddie rolled down the car window and threw an orange at the cat, who jumped into the air and took off running. Then he remembered that he was after the photographer and those boys, not a cat with a white stripe down its mangy back.

"We'll take care of them," Freddie said of Uncle, Hector, and Mando. "I don't like when someone snitches, especially on us."

"Me neither," Huey agreed. "Then we'll get our money and leave, right?"

The money from the armored-car robbery was stored in an abandoned barn east of Fresno. After they took care of that photographer and his do-gooder kids, Freddie figured that they would drive to Los Angeles and take a flight to Minneapolis, Huey's hometown. Huey wanted to be with his mother for the Winter Olympics.

"We'll watch the ski jumping," Freddie said. "I like it when they crash."

"Not a bad idea," Huey agreed.

Soon after they had eaten their oranges, a Ford came up the road, its headlights cutting through the light fog. Smirking, Freddie looked at Huey and said, "It's them, the snitches."

"How do you know?"

"It's a photographer's car. Cheap."

The Ford Escort smoked and rattled as it pulled into the driveway of the Inouye farm. Freddie saw three heads, two of them belonging to children. He saw them and took his cigarette-lighter pistol out of the small Italian-designed holster that he had bought in San Francisco with counterfeit twenty-dollar bills. He pulled the trigger and a tongue of flame shot out. "This'll scare those blabbermouth punk kids."

But after a moment of thought Freddie came up with a better plan, something even more violent. He wanted to run them off the road, slam that Ford into one of the trees. That way he'd teach them what happens to blabbermouths. He turned on the car's engine and warmed the car. The windows began to fog from their breathing. Huey placed his hands in front of the heater and rubbed them. "I'm cold, Freddie."

"Not as cold as you'll be in a prison cell, if we don't do this right." As soon as the windows were defrosted, Huey turned off the engine. Freddie looked at his watch, also bought with counterfeit bills, made a face, and said, "They're taking too long." He shrugged and waited staring straight ahead, meanness living in each dark pupil. Neither of them said anything. After twenty minutes they saw the Ford Escort come out of the driveway, two German shepherds barking at the wheels. Huey turned on his engine and waited for Freddie's signal.

"Go ahead," Freddie said simply.

"Here goes," Huey said and, throwing the last orange slice into his mouth, shifted the car from park to drive. He pulled over to the side of the road and picked up speed, scaring the German shepherds. The Buick moved next to the Ford Escort. Freddie rolled down the window, grinning menacingly at Uncle, whose eyes spread wide with shock.

"Slam them!" Freddie ordered.

Huey steered the Buick toward the Ford. The cars slammed, sparks kicking between the grinding of two fenders. The scrape of metal was earsplitting. Huey grimaced at the sound and wished it were over.

Freddie laughed and said, "That's the way. Get closer."

Huey yanked the steering wheel right and the cars slammed hard, jolting both Freddie and Huey. "Good job!" Freddie laughed. He could see steam rising from the Ford and noticed that a door handle had fallen off and the windshield was cracked.

Huey pressed the Buick against the Ford a third time. They were so close that Freddie reached out his hand and tried to grab Uncle's hair. But Uncle dodged his hand and slammed Freddie's face with the heel of his palm.

"Ouch!" Freddie screamed as he sat back into his seat, holding his nose. He blew into a Kleenex and saw flecks of blood. Really mad now, he shook his fist and told Huey, "Get close to that punk!"

Huey maneuvered the car next to the Ford, which was wrapped in steam and buckled like a trash can. Freddie could see one of the boys holding up a camera and taking pictures. This made him even madder.

"Ram 'em hard," Freddie shouted. "They make me sick!"

Huey threw the steering a hard right and their car smashed against the Ford. The Ford's left front tire exploded and it went flying into an orange tree.

The Buick pulled away and disappeared into the valley fog.

CHAPTER 9

Hector climbed out the side of the car that was not buckled. He was dazed, not so much from being hurt but from the roller-coaster-like ride that brought them to a halt in the orange grove. He brushed aside a limb of the orange tree that they had knocked over. He could smell the oranges that the tires had crushed and the chemical scent of the grove. And every time he took a step he could feel the sucking action of the mud under his shoes. He walked to the middle of the road to stomp the mud from his feet. He looked up the road white with fog. The car that had rammed them was gone.

"*Híjole*, what a ride," Mando said as he climbed out of the car and wobbled as if he had just gotten off the Tilt-o-Whirl. "I feel dizzy."

Uncle came out of the car. "Everyone okay?" he asked in a frightened tone.

"I'm fine," Hector said as he went over and

examined one of the tires. He put a pinkie into a gaping hole that had drained the life out of the tire.

"I'm okay," Mando said. "I jus' hurt my shoulder or something. I'll be all right."

Hector rose, slapping dirt from his hands and walked to the front of the car. Steam was rising from the hood. He opened it and all three of them looked at the engine. Flecks of green coolant were splattered everywhere.

Holding his nose with his hand, the stinky odor of steam getting to him, Uncle reached his other hand down and poked at the radiator hose. "It's just split. It's nothin' big."

He stepped back and examined the battered car. The driver's side was crushed. The glass was busted into spider lines and lightning-like cracks. Streaks of red paint from the Buick were embedded into the paint of the Ford.

"I never did like the color," he quipped. "The red does something for it." He tried to pull the door open, but the handle came off in his hand. He tossed it into the orange grove. He sucked in a lot of country air and asked Hector, "Did you get a picture of them?"

"Yeah, dozens," Hector answered. When he saw that the Buick had meant business, Hector had reached into the back seat, took his uncle's camera, ripped off the lens cap, and shot a rapid succession of pictures, unsure if they were focused.

"I hope you got a picture of me smacking that guy," Uncle said. He looked at the heel of his palm. It still tingled from the upper cut.

"I hope so, too. You were *bad*, Unc. Mando, did you see Unc whack him one?"

"How could I, *ese*? I was down on the floor prayin'."

Mr. Inouye, with one of his two German shepherds, stepped toward them out of the fog. "I heard some terrible noise," he said as he shook his head and ran a finger along the side of the Ford. "Ruined a good car. Are you fellas okay?"

"We're okay," Hector said. He touched the cold nose of the dog that came to nuzzle him. Orange pulp was still stuck to the German shepherd's nose.

Mr. Inouye walked around the car and moaned when he saw his fallen tree. He picked an orange and tossed it. The German shepherd ran after it in great leaps. "Oh, this is bad," groaned the farmer.

"Don't worry, Mr. Inouye. I have insurance," Uncle said.

"I'm not worried about insurance. I'm speaking of the fog. I think it's getting worse every year."

"It wasn't the fog," Hector said. "Some guys tried to run us off the road!"

They returned to the farm. While Hector and Mando went inside, after taking off their muddy shoes, Mr. Inouye helped Uncle replace the radiator hose and change the tire.

"You have a nice house," Hector said, trying to make conversation with Mrs. Inouye. They were sitting on stools in the kitchen, eating cookies. A small TV was on, the volume turned down so low that the voices sounded like gnats.

"Yes, it's a nice crib," Mando said as he looked around.

"What do you mean by 'crib'?" a confused Mrs. Inouye asked.

"You know, 'crib' means a house."

"Mando, that's no way to talk," Hector scolded. He turned to Mrs. Inouye and politely explained. "We live in Los Angeles, and we hardly got any room."

"But Los Angeles is so pretty," said Mrs. Inouye.

Hector and Mando looked at each, as if to say, "It is?" They lived in East Los, where the rows of houses were cramped and cars often parked on the sidewalk. Graffiti slashed across walls. Litter blew across the streets, and broken wine bottles glittered in the gutter. Across the street there was a *panadería* that did good business. All day and all night its pastry sweetened the air, but the smell was sickening after a while.

"Mr. Paul says hi," Hector said, undoing the top of an Oreo and looking at the white cream. He thought of hooking his front teeth into the cream, but he knew it would be impolite.

"You mean Paul Kanzaki?" Mrs. Inouye said with a bright smile.

"I think that's him," Hector said, nibbling his cookie like a rabbit.

"Yeah, it's him," Mando said. He jumped up from his stool and took a business card from his pocket. "I got it when we left his shop." He handed it to a smiling Mrs. Inouye.

"How is he?" Mrs. Inouye asked, her elbows up on the counter, fully interested.

"He's okay, I guess. He colored the picture of your farm."

"He did? How nice." Mrs. Inouye got up and went to the living room and brought back the picture that she had already propped on her wide-screen television. "He did a nice job."

The three of them were admiring the framed picture when Mr. Inouye came into the kitchen wearing his leather work gloves. "Boys, your uncle wants you."

Hector and Mando thanked Mrs. Inouye for the cookies, put on their mud-caked shoes at the back door, and left the house. The beat-up Ford was in the driveway, the German shepherds sniffing the new tire.

Hector and Mando got in. Uncle gave a thumbs-up sign and said, "It's still working."

They drove the rattling Ford from the Inouye farm back to Parlier. Uncle stopped at the convenience store and asked if they had seen two men in a red Buick.

"Earlier," the woman replied. She had a trail of tears tattooed near her left eye. Her other eye was bloodshot.

"Can you describe them?" Uncle asked.

"Just two guys. One fat one. Thin hair. Maybe forty-five, fifty. I saw that one had plenty of bills in his wallet, and I'm not talking about one-dollar bills, either."

Uncle backed away from the counter, and with his brow pinched with worry and his leg feeling stiff, he limped to the potato chip rack. "You guys want some Fritos?"

"It's them, huh, Uncle?" Hector asked.

"Yeah, it's them, all right. You don't want a bag?"

"Nah."

They got back into the car and returned to Fresno. They took the old highway because Uncle was afraid the car would come apart if they tried the freeway. The door rattled and the glass vibrated loudly. Instead of going directly back to the apartment, Uncle stopped at Paul's studio. The bums were still in front of the building. Now they were sitting on cardboard, sucking on another bottle, pink-colored wine this time.

"Good afternoon," one of them slurred. "What happened to your car?"

Uncle waved but didn't say anything. The three of them went inside the studio. Paul was in the back taking a family portrait—father and mother and four children in clothes that were ironed so well the creases were sharp as knives.

The three of them tiptoed into the photo shoot. Uncle waved to get Paul's attention. Paul had his back to them. He was tickling a girl's chin so that he could get a smile on her sullen face. Finally Uncle whispered, "Hey, Paul, can I use your lab?"

Uncle didn't want to return to his apartment, not just yet. Since Paul's darkroom was all set up, he figured it would be easier to develop the film there. He was dying to see who the guys were.

Paul squinted in their direction, hand over his brow in salute as the studio lights beamed in his eyes. "Julio?" he asked. "Is that you?"

"Yeah, it's me. Can we use your darkroom?"

"Go ahead. *Mi darkroom es tu darkroom.*"

They went into the little room, Hector and Mando feeling like old pros. They helped Uncle mix chemicals and fix the timer. Using metal tongs, Uncle dipped the unrolled film into the solution and rocked the pan as the timer clicked. Slowly the images emerged. Some were blurry and strange-looking, like a TV out of focus. One was a jarring image of the Ford's ceiling. Another was of Uncle with his eyes closed and another was of Mando's left ear.

"Here's one," Uncle said. The negative lay on the bottom of the pan, but the image deepened and became clear—Freddie grinning menacingly at them. Uncle brought it out of the solution with tongs and remarked, "Damn, he's ugly."

CHAPTER 10

After they drove from the Inouye farm, Freddie Bork and Huey "Crybaby" Walker returned to Fresno. They took the freeway, careful not to speed. They had the radio on, listening for reports of the armored-car robbery. But none came on. Mostly they heard the jingles of commercials advertising after valentine's specials, which reminded Freddie that he hadn't gotten his mother a card for Valentine's Day.

"You think we got 'em? It went right for a tree," Huey said. Both hands were on the wheel, knuckles white as bone. He was worried now and beginning to wonder if he would see the Winter Olympics after all.

"I hope so," Freddie said. He popped a knuckle and rubbed the nub of his pinkie. "That kid had a camera. I think maybe he took a picture."

"That's not good."

They both shivered at the thought of going to

prison. Freddie had once served six months for mail fraud and Huey a year for grand theft. They both got off for good behavior and then immediately used that goodness to hold up an elderly woman's yard sale in Porterville. They got away with eighty-five dollars and a set of pots and pans.

"We're going to have to get those photos," Freddie said. "We'll dump this car and get another one."

"Do we have to?" Huey asked. "I was starting to like this one." He admired the dash and nice styling.

"Yeah," Freddie lamented. "It does have nice lines."

They drove to Fresno and parked in a red zone near the downtown library. They wiped the steering wheel free of fingerprints and left the keys in the ignition with the windows rolled down. They crossed the street and decided to have lunch. Their breakfast of waffles, sausages, and eggs had been put to good use. It was a little after one o'clock, though the clock on the wall, batteries dead, said it was four-thirty. The place was dead, too. The restaurant was empty except for a couple near the back. They were holding hands and cooing at each other.

The waitress was sitting down, smoking a cigarette and looking bored. "Have any seat you want," she said. She turned and yelled, "Enrique, get the grill going."

Freddie and Huey sat near the window that looked out over the library. The Buick was still there.

Freddie took the plastic-covered menu from the napkin holder. He opened it and asked Huey. "Whatta you gonna have?"

"Burger and fries."

"I thought you were watching your weight."

"I am. I'm gettin' it without cheese."

The waitress came up to the table. She smelled of smoke and crispy bacon. "What is it going to be, fellas?"

Huey ordered his burger and fries, along with a diet Dr Pepper, and Freddie asked, "Do you make your own soup here?"

"No, it comes from a can."

"Is the fish fresh?"

"No, we got 'em frozen."

"Is the orange juice fresh?"

"No, that comes from a can, too."

Freddie clicked his tongue and ordered, "Gimme a tuna melt. Make the tuna real."

The waitress scribbled in her pad and left coughing.

"Some waitress," Freddie remarked and gazed out the window. A guy on a bicycle was circling their Buick. He whizzed by and then stopped. He looked around and, seeing no one, placed his bicycle against the meter and got into the car. He immediately started the engine and took off with a screech.

"No class," Freddie said. "The guy could have pulled away smooth." He drank from his water glass and smacked his lips. "That tastes good." He looked directly at Huey and, nervously twisting the ring on his hairy finger, moaned, "This is real delicate. We're gonna have to break into the photographer's pad. We gotta get those photos."

"Do we have to?"

"Yeah, we do."

"I'm scared," Huey said as he tied his napkin into a noose. "Don't you think we should get out of town?"

"We'll be gone by tomorrow. Scouts' honor, Huey." Freddie held up two pudgy fingers, smiling.

When the waitress returned with ketchup and mustard, they fell silent, and remained silent until the food was served. The french fries were burnt and looked like bark from a tree. The burger was greasy. The tuna melt was skimpy, as if the chef had scraped a tuna can with a fork. But they dug in, faces close to the plates.

"Let's get another American car," Huey suggested, a french fry hanging from the corner of his mouth.

"Yeah, I like what GM's doing. They're catching up with the Japanese." His tuna melt came with a pickle and a pinch of potato chips, mostly flakes no bigger than fingernails.

They sighed and ate everything that was served. When they left, a batch of free matches in their hands, Freddie paid with a counterfeit bill. He waved to the waitress who was back in her chair lost in a cloud of smoke.

CHAPTER 11

U ncle and the boys left Paul's studio and returned to the apartment, the Ford heaving
a fit of steam as it rounded the final block. Uncle's landlord, Dr. Femur the chiropractor, was
raking leaves. He was bundled in two sweaters,
both the very color of the leaves he was raking.
A pipe hung from his mouth, dead of smoke
and fire. He waved at them, walked over gin-
gerly, and asked, "What happened to your car,
Julio?"

"A little accident. No one was hurt," Uncle
answered as he got out of the passenger's side.
He opened the hood and through the steam saw
that the radiator clamp had loosened.

The chiropractor walked around the car, mum-
bling and sucking his pipe. He turned to Hector.
"So this is your nephew?"

"Yeah, this is Hector and this is Mando. This
is Dr. Femur."

"Hi," the boys said and shook Dr. Femur's
hand that was cold with a river of bluish veins.

The chiropractor examined them closely. His pipe now out of his mouth, he smacked his lips, and exclaimed, "I've seen your face before." He pointed his pipe at Mando. "And yours, too."

"We were in the paper this morning," Hector volunteered with a bright smile, happy to be recognized. "In the 'Today's Youth' column."

"Oh, and I suppose you read about that terrible robbery. The world's going to the dogs," the chiropractor remarked. He fumbled for a wooden match from his sweater pocket and struck it against the car fender. "Those fellas who were driving the armored truck, I bet, are a bundle of nerves. I would crack their bones for free, if they asked. The body can't take that kind of shock."

"Yes, it was real bad," Uncle said and prodded the boys toward his upstairs apartment. "Excuse us, Dr. Femur."

The chiropractor waved and said with good intention. "Stay out of trouble, boys. It's a terrible world."

It's starting to look that way, Hector thought to himself. The last time he had been so worried was when he was twelve years old. For fun he started his mother's Toyota and then, somehow, locked himself out. The engine ran a full tank to almost empty. When his mother came home from the market and discovered the car idling, she sat down on the front steps and cried into her groceries. She thought her son was turning into a juvenile delinquent.

Once upstairs in Uncle Julio's apartment Hector stripped off his jacket, turned on the floor furnace using a pair of pliers, and asked, "Uncle, can I play the answering machine?"

"Good idea," Uncle said, kicking off his shoes. His feet were frozen.

Hector pushed the replay and a woman's voice began, "Is Rick there? I want to talk to Rick! Tell him to call me, 'cause if he doesn't he's going to hate life!"

Hector shivered at the threat. He thought for a moment that it might be good to have that woman on his side.

A second beep sounded and a message began with grizzly laughter, then a man's oily voice that breathed, "Hey kiddies, how's it going? You doin' good in school? Heh heh, heh. Julio, we're going to break your face and then your camera, or maybe your camera first and then your face. How do you like them apples? Heh, heh, heh."

Hector looked at his Uncle, who had paled at the threat. He nodded his head at the floor and bit his lip. Julio had known threats in the past. Once, when he was working in Los Angeles, a boyfriend of one of his clients — runner-up for Miss Auto Parts of Gardena — circled his apartment for days with three baseball bats sticking out of the window of a ratty Volkswagen. He was upset because his girlfriend hadn't won and he blamed Julio's photography.

Hector threw himself on the couch. "Man, we need Bertha Sanchez. She could help us." Hector figured that she was probably pressing some boy's face like a cookie cutter into the playground grass.

"Yeah, Bertha," Mando said wearily.

"Whatta you gonna do?" Hector asked Uncle.

Before he could answer there was a knock at the door. All three of them jumped and yelled, "*¡Ay, Dios!*"

Hector tiptoed to the window. He parted the curtain and peeked down but didn't see anyone. The knock came a second time, this time harder. "It's your landlord, Unc," Hector said when he looked a second time. "I'll get it." Hector ran downstairs, unlatched the door, and greeted him with a "hi."

"Sorry to bother you," the chiropractor said and nervously unfolded a newspaper. "But would you sign your column for me?"

"What?"

"Your column."

"*¿En serio?* Are you serious?"

Mando had come down and joined Hector. He asked, "*¿Qué pasa?* What's up?"

"I want to send the article to my nephew," the chiropractor said. He took a pen from his sweater pocket. "You too," he said to Mando. "See, my nephew is in a correctional facility in Tulare. I was thinking that it would be good for him to see how you two are turning out so fine. Could inspire him."

Hector glanced over at Mando, but didn't say anything. He paused for a second and asked the chiropractor, "What's he in for?"

"He stole a car." He clicked his pen and thrust it at Hector. "Here, I'm sure it would brighten his day."

"What's his name?" Hector asked.

"Derek — but his friends call him Exterminator. Could you say something nice?"

"Okay." Hector, lips pursed, wrote, "We're waiting for you to get out, Exterminator" and realized immediately that Derek might take it wrong. He then added: "Very soon." Hector signed his name with plenty of looping action.

Mando signed his name, "*su carnal de East Los*, Armando Hernandez de Lopez Tafolla, the first and only."

"He'll appreciate this," the chiropractor said. "If you need your bones cracked and realigned, just come see me." He winked at Hector and Mando and left with the newspaper folded under his arm.

"Who was that?" Uncle asked when the boys came back upstairs.

"It's hard to explain," Hector said, "but I think Dr. Femur thinks we're celebrities. We might be if these robbers catch us."

"The *vato* says that he could crack our bones," Mando asked.

"He's a chiropractor," Uncle explained. "He's a doctor who realigns your spine."

"Great," Hector sighed. "Looks like we might need him."

"I need him now," Uncle said while he rubbed the back of his neck. "Maybe I'll go down and get my neck twisted."

When the telephone rang, they jumped again. Hector answered and heard Ms. Moreno's voice.

"Oh, hi," Hector said happily. She asked if he liked the article and photograph. "Sure made us popular," he answered. "People are even asking for autographs." When she asked for Uncle, Hector held up the telephone and screamed, "It's your *ruca*."

"Hey, you little *cholo*, be cool," Uncle said mildly embarrassed. He took the telephone and said in a soft silky voice, "Julio speaking." He smiled into the telephone. His eyes became smoky with romance. "Dinner at seven. Charming . . ."

Hector nearly gagged. He left his uncle in privacy and went to the kitchen, where Mando was looking in the refrigerator.

"Is your uncle on a diet?" Mando asked. "There's nothin' 'cept the Super Bowl salad and an old apple. I'll take the salad."

"You're exaggerating," Hector responded.

They brought out a half gallon carton of milk and fixed themselves a bowl of Captain Crunch. They sat down on the couch. Hector held up the negatives to the light. He studied the robbers' faces and then handed them to Mando. "Man, they have faces only their mothers could love."

Mando studied the negatives and then put them down.

"In a little bit, let's go down and ask Dr. Femur to break our bones," Hector said.

Mando laughed at that, laughed so hard that milk squirted from his nostrils. "Okay," he said, "but you go first."

CHAPTER 12

Freddie Bork and Huey "Crybaby" Walker cruised up and down Uncle's block. They were driving a new used car, an Oldsmobile with a CD player, which they had stolen from a car dealer on Blackstone Avenue. Immediately they bought some CD's and paid in counterfeit bills.

"This is real comfy," Freddie said in a whisper as he eased the Oldsmobile to the curb. He cut the engine. The music, a Garth Brooks song about roping cows, died in the speakers.

"That second-rate photographer must live over the garage," Freddie said, "not the house." He studied the large ranch-style house, as he planned their attack. He then grinned happily when he spotted Dr. Femur's chiropractor's sign. "And here's the deal, Huey. Your back's out of whack and we're gonna get it fixed."

"It is?" Huey asked. He was staring dreamily at the Garth Brooks CD, wondering if it felt great to be famous.

"You're gonna get a tune-up from the chiropractor," Freddie said as he opened the car. "Let's go."

They got out of the car and crossed the street. Freddie glanced at the mailbox on the road. He saw "Julio Silva, Photographer," on one of the boxes and almost did a jig of happiness.

"We're gonna get these punks," Freddie said angrily. "Come on, Huey, hobble a little."

"What's hobble?"

"You don't know the word hobble? Whatta you, dumb?" Freddie hunched his shoulders and let his hands go limp. He walked in a circle like a gorilla. He straightened up and said, "You got it? H-o-b-b-l-e. That's hobble."

"I got it, Freddie. You're good at explaining," Huey said and, with Freddie leading the way, hobbled toward the house. They knocked. The chiropractor answered the door, his pipe hanging from his mouth. One of his two sweaters was off, and he was skinny as a skeleton.

"Sorry to bother you, doc," Freddie said. "But my friend's got a back problem."

Huey grinned in pain. He moaned and stuttered, "I-I-I hurt real bad."

"Come in. Let's see," the chiropractor said, and showed the two inside the house that was overly warm. "I'm Dr. Femur."

"I'm Demetrius Armstrong," Freddie said.

"I'm J.J. Cool," Huey said.

91

"This way," Dr. Femur said and led Freddie and a hobbling Huey to a small office connected to his house. In the corner of the office hung a human skeleton, jaw slack and grinning with a perfect set of yellowish teeth. On the wall hung profiles of people with swaybacks, slumped shoulders, hunched backs, bowlegs, pigeon-toed stances — people in a lot of pain and hating life.

"Nice office," Freddie said. "Real clean like."

"It is quite comfortable," the chiropractor agreed with obvious pleasure. "It's convenient to work at home."

Huey was told to climb onto a table, facedown. The chiropractor ran his hands up and down Huey's spine, first softly and then with great vigor. His bones popped like buttons and he moaned, "Man, that feels good."

Freddie walked over to the skeleton. He worked its jaw so its mouth opened and closed.

"J.J.," the skeleton said. "J.J., this is going to be you if you don't get those photos."

Huey glanced over at Freddie and the skeleton. "That's not funny."

The chiropractor placed his hands around Huey's head, and gave it a snapping jerk to the left. The muscles popped and again Huey moaned from ticklish delight.

"Break his neck. Give it a good twist," the

skeleton shouted. Freddie clacked its jaws together and laughed.

"That's not funny," Huey said. He moaned again when the chiropractor gave it a jerk to the right.

Freddie let the skeleton's jaw drop. Now serious, he asked the chiropractor, "I see that you have a photographer living in your apartment. The one on top of the garage."

"Yes, that's right," the chiropractor said. He gave Huey's neck such a twist that Freddie squinted and asked, "You okay, Huey? I mean, J.J."

"Feels great. You should go next."

Freddie ignored the suggestion and returned his attention to the chiropractor. "We need some photos taken," Freddie said. "You think he's home — I think his name is Silva."

"Yes, that's right. Julio Silva."

"Is he good?"

"I can vouch for him. He took those photographs on the wall."

Freddie didn't bother to look. "We don't want to disturb his family, but do you think he would mind if we dropped in on him?"

"No. I don't believe so. He has his nephew staying with him this weekend." Dr. Femur turned Huey on his back and worked on his stomach, pushing his fist into his abdomen. Huey let out a chuckle and said, "Stop. I'm ticklish." The doctor ignored him and remarked, "The nephew was in the newspaper. In the youth column. He and his friend were responsible for taking pictures of the armored-car robbers."

"Is that right?" Freddie said. "It's a cryin' shame about all the crime these days."

Huey stopped chuckling and was now worried.

"All right, enough with J.J.," Freddie said. "Give me a rubdown, doc."

Freddie lay down on the table and the chiropractor began to pop every bone in his tension-stiff neck. He worked his spine like a zipper, up and down, up and down. Freddie groaned and then rose feeling great.

"How much, doc?" Freddie asked, bringing out his wallet from the back of his pants.

"You seem like nice fellas," he said writing out a receipt. "How 'bout forty altogether."

Freddie opened his wallet and brought out three counterfeit twenty-dollar bills. He handed them to Dr. Femur and said, "Please, take this. I'm so glad my friend is no longer hobbling."

Huey straightened his posture, good as new.

They left the office and returned to the front door. They shook hands and thanked the doctor.

As they were about to leave there was a knock on the door.

"Looks like you have more clients," Freddie said.

When the chiropractor opened the door, he discovered Hector and Mando standing together, smiling.

"Oh, it's my friends," the chiropractor said with a genuine pleasure. "Please come in."

"We thought we'd come by," Hector said as he wiped his shoes and entered. "You know, have our bones broken."

The chiropractor laughed at the expression. To Freddie and Huey, he said, "Well, good-bye, gentlemen. You see that I'm keeping busy."

Freddie and Huey's glare fell on the two boys. Hector and Mando both seemed to know Freddie's face, but from where, they both wondered.

Freddie thought of grabbing the two right there, but he knew that it would be the wrong move. He would take care of them later, wring their necks like squealing chickens and throw them from their new used Oldsmobile.

"Yes, it's your turn," Freddie sneered at Hector as he passed through the front door. "It's your turn to have your neck broken."

CHAPTER 13

Only after the front door closed did Hector recognize the face of Freddie Bork, the robber in the negative — square face, thinning hair, and teeth that were small and sharp, the kind that were good for tearing into meat. He gulped and swallowed with fear. He turned to Mando, who seemed unaware of what had just happened.

"It's *him*," Hector hissed. "The dude!"

"The dude?" a confused Mando said. "What dude?"

Hector spun around and raced to the front window in the living room, nearly knocking over a lamp. He looked out, hands cupped over his brow. Freddie and Huey were crossing the street in a hurry.

"Come on!" Hector beckoned loudly.

"What's going on?" Dr. Femur asked.

Hector didn't have time to explain. He raced out of the house and to the street, legs kicking high as he ran through a pile of raked leaves.

The Oldsmobile was already down the street, the taillights winking red as the car braked softly and turned a corner.

Hector slapped his thighs in disappointment. "Oh, man, they know where we live."

"*¿Quién?*" asked Mando as he pulled up next to Hector.

"The robber! The guy in the negative."

"No way, Hector. *Chále, ese.*"

But Hector was more than sure. The man was too ugly not to be sure. He shivered at what the robber had said — "It's your turn to have your neck broken." Once, in fourth grade, Hector had broken his arm while playing basketball. The pain was enough to make him cry in front of three girls, including his girlfriend, who later left him for a fifth-grader with a pierced ear. Now it appeared his whole body would be broken. He imagined with a cringe how much that would hurt.

They hurried back to the apartment. Uncle was lounging on the couch viewing the negatives, a cup of coffee between his legs.

"Unc," Hector yelled. "I just saw the dude. The one in the negative."

At first, it didn't register in Uncle Julio's mind what Hector was saying. Then suddenly he yelled "What?" and jumped to his feet, spilling his coffee, a stain immediately darkening the front of his pants. The negatives dropped to the floor, a sprinkle of coffee raining on them.

"He was over there," Hector said, waving vaguely in the direction of Dr. Femur's house.

"Dr. Femur's?"

Hector and Mando nodded their heads. Hector explained that he and Mando were going to take up the chiropractor's offer for a little body work. They had entered the house and the guy was smiling at them. But it was not a nice smile, Hector explained. It was mean and ugly. He could see the man's teeth were packed with food.

Uncle sighed and paced, head down, muttering to himself, "How did he find us?" He limped over to the kitchen for a dish towel and began dabbing the front of his pants.

"I don't know, Unc."

The telephone rang, and all three jumped. On the fourth ring, right before the message machine kicked in, Uncle answered the telephone.

"Hey, Stewart?" Uncle said with relief. He picked up a pen and started doodling on the message pad. "We have another job?" Uncle's smiling face darkened as the conversation continued. "That's good, that's good," he repeated and then hung up the telephone. He gazed despondently at the boys. His eyes were dead of any kind of light. "Stewart told 'em."

"He told the robbers where you lived?" Hector said, arms dropping to his side in defeat.

"It's not his fault. He didn't know," Uncle explained in a hush. "He said they were farmers looking for a photographer."

"We should call the *policía*," Hector suggested.

"We'll do it later, after dinner," Uncle answered. He didn't want to wreck the evening. He figured he had a chance for his last supper with Vicky Moreno, a cause for joy in his grief. He had the evening to look forward to. After that, he mused, he might just be a dead photographer with a Nikon 3 tied around his neck. Uncle turned and said, "Hey, don't let this get us down. We have a dinner to go to."

While Hector and Mando showered, Uncle remembered the unclamped water hose. He fixed the problem with wire and a T-shirt torn into strips, and then drove to the automatic teller to get sixty dollars, the last of his money. He returned, showered until the grime under his fingernails disappeared, and dressed in good clothes. He was feeling pretty happy. He put on an old Santana album and sang along, beating a rhythm on the bed. But he took off his shirt after he stood in front of the mirror, full face and then profile, and saw that his shirt was sloppily ironed. He ironed the shirt again and put it back on, the warmth sending a herd of goosebumps racing up his arms. He smoothed his face with the cologne called Lover Boy and then slapped his face so that a little red blossomed on his cheeks.

Hector and Mando snickered playfully at Uncle, who ignored them and said, "You don't know what love is."

It was almost six when they left the apartment. They rattled out of the yard in their buckled Ford Escort. They looked nervously about the street, but didn't see the robbers' car. They pulled out of the driveway and drove two blocks in silence before Hector pounded on the radio. A bass-thumping country song called "Robbers in the Night" blared in the speakers.

They drove to Vicky Moreno's house, a new tract home in north Fresno. Even at night, they could see that the lawn was mowed and everything was tidy. Even the garden hose was rolled up neatly.

"Be cool, you little *vatos*," Uncle warned as he rang the doorbell. "And don't order too much. I only got sixty bucks."

"Man, I'm hungry," Hector announced, touching his stomach. "You hungry, Mando?"

"Yeah, man. I didn't have anything but Captain Crunch for lunch."

Vicky Moreno answered the door. She was in a flowered dress and a bouquet of perfume hovered about her. Her hair was full of tight curls.

"Hello," she sang. "Please come in."

The three wiped their shoes like bulls and entered her house which, like her lawn and garden, was tidy. Roses stood tall in a Chinese vase. The appliquéd pillows were propped up on the sofa. The walls were hung with paintings and photographs of Mexico. Light rock music played in a far room.

"You look stunning, like a night of a thousand and one stars," Julio said, not wasting time. His eyes sparkled and his chest puffed out like a rooster.

Hector looked down at his shoes. He bit his lip and thought of Bertha Sanchez in order to keep from laughing. His uncle, he thought, was coming on too strong, and they hadn't even gotten out of the house. He had to wonder what he would sound like after he had a glass of wine.

"Thank you, Julio," answered Ms. Moreno. "I'll just get my purse and we'll go."

After she left the room, Uncle wheeled around and said, "Nice pad, ¿qué no? A little trendy, but hey, the color scheme's cool. He bent, sniffed a rose in the vase, and sneezed. "I guess I'm not used to nice things."

"Is she rich?" Mando asked.

"If she's a reporter, I doubt it. Must have some money in the family somewhere." He paused for a second and added, "I wonder how you can get into the family?"

Vicky returned with her handbag, and the four left the house. As they walked toward the Ford, Uncle nervously began to explain that they had a little trouble and some parts of the car didn't work.

"A little trouble," bewildered Vicky said as she stopped in her tracks and stared at the car. "What happened?"

Uncle shrugged his shoulders. He went around to the driver's side and then realized that he didn't have a door handle. "Oops," he smiled. "It's gone."

"Gone?" Vicky asked with surprise.

"Oh, we just ran into a tree. Unc wasn't drunk or anything," Hector said.

"Hey, Hector, don't give Vicky the wrong impression," he said smiling as he squeezed the back of Hector's neck, hard.

Hector, shoulders hunched and giggling, said, "Okay, Unc."

They piled into the car, with Hector and Mando in the back and Uncle Julio and Vicky in the front.

They rolled out of the driveway and up the street.

"Watch this," Hector said to Vicky. He leaned forward between Uncle and Vicky and slammed the car radio with the heel of his palm. Country-western music began playing, a song about a cow roped by moonlight.

"How ingenious," Vicky remarked.

"It's a one-station radio," Hector added. He turned the knob from left to right and the same song blared.

Uncle took a hand off the steering wheel and placed it around Hector's face. Without looking, he gave it a push. Hector went flying backwards, his throat filled with laughter.

Vicky turned and smiled at the boys. "I hope you enjoyed the article."

"It's made us a lot of friends," Hector said facetiously.

"Yeah, we even signed it for this dude in juvie," Mando said.

"Oh," Vicky commented, her earrings jingling a tune.

"Me and Hector were in juvie once," Mando said, elbowing Hector. "Huh, Hector?"

"That's right. We were locked out of the house and had to break in."

"Chill the topic," Uncle said, adjusting the rearview mirror on Hector's smirking face. "You don't want to give Vicky the idea that we're crummy people."

They drove in silence. The sweetest smell was Vicky and the strangest was Unc's Lover Boy cologne. Their scents clashed and would have made a mess of the evening except the back window of their Ford station wagon fell out and shattered as they maneuvered around the corner on Cedar Avenue.

Vicky screamed, "What happened?"

Uncle braked, screaming, "What the hell!"

Hector, quickly up on his knees and looking back, said, "Unc, the back window fell out." Under the street lights, a river of glass glittered.

"Like I said, the car's falling apart," Uncle said as he put the car into gear and took off, his eyes on the rearview mirror. Cold air flapped through the car. It stirred up loose pages of newspaper, mussed up Vicky's hair, and peeled off the sweetness from her skin.

CHAPTER 14

Freddie and Huey sat in their motel room, the cable TV on and blaring a movie. Freddie chugged on a bottle of Pepto-Bismol and groaned, "I knew we shouldn't have eaten at that restaurant." He shook the bottle and took a second, deeper swig.

"I thought the food was good," Huey said with his eyes on the screen of the television.

"If you barf it'll make you feel better," Huey said. "Really works."

"Please, Huey, I'm already sick to my stomach," Freddie complained. He sat on the bed and let his eyes fall once again on an article in a late edition of the newspaper. The article was about them and their Chevy Caprice.

"Here's the deal," Freddie said, recapping the bottle. "Huey, are you listening?"

"Yeah, I'm listening," Huey answered, his eyes riveted to the screen. He bit into a Baby Ruth candy bar and chewed slowly.

"We're going back tonight. We're going to get

those negatives." Freddie stood up, his hand on his aching stomach. "We're gonna make those kids pay."

Freddie explained that they would get the negatives, push the kids around some, tie the uncle in small knots, and then get out of town with their stash of new money. He said he wanted to get to Minnesota in time to relax at Huey's mother's house and watch the Winter Olympics.

Freddie turned off the television.

"Hey, the good part was coming," Huey complained.

"No, this is the good part," Freddie argued. "Get your coat and let's go."

But before they drove to Uncle's, Freddie instructed Huey to drive past the restaurant where they had eaten lunch. Freddie rolled down the window and hurled the half-empty bottle of Pepto-Bismol at the front window. The plate-glass window came down in jagged sheets, shattering on the sidewalk. Freddie rolled up the window, burped, and said, "I feel better already."

CHAPTER 15

"Dessert? Sure, why not?" Hector agreed when the waiter returned with a dessert menu. He threw down his starched napkin, smeared with plum sauce and beef Wellington, and patted his taut stomach. He gazed smiling at his uncle, who shot a stern look at his nephew. Hector then recalled that his uncle had only sixty dollars, and the restaurant that Vicky suggested came with two chandeliers, three waiters per table, a tier of candles, real china and silver, a string quartet, row upon row of French wines, and — despite the embarrassment of their rattling Ford — valet parking. The attendant parked it behind a Dumpster.

"On second thought," Hector said, calling back the waiter. "I'm pretty full. I have some popcorn balls at home. Me and Mando will just snack on them later."

The waiter left with the dessert menu under his arm. The conversation continued where it had left off: soccer. Seeing that everyone was

107

interested — or at least was not yawning — Hector bragged mildly about how many goals he'd made.

"Yeah, everything is true," Mando said, backing up his friend. "He's the best player at school."

Hector beamed and bit back a smile.

"Enough of soccer," Uncle said, now turning on his silky voice. "Vicky doesn't want to hear about soccer." He gazed longingly at Vicky, who was warming up to Uncle. "Why don't you *chamacos* take a walk in the mall?"

All evening he had complimented Vicky with such comments as "your article in the newspaper was swell," "fish is my favorite food," "I like the buttons on your dress," and "You're a tidy woman" — small talk that made Hector wonder how his uncle ever got girlfriends.

"But I didn't tell Vicky about when we played Hollenbeck Junior High," Hector said. He lowered his head and saw that he had plum sauce spotted on the front of his shirt. He thought of scraping away the stain, but that would be poor form.

Uncle shot him another hard look.

"All right, we'll take a walk," Hector said. But before he scooted out of their booth, Hector reached discreetly into his pocket and slipped his uncle a twenty-dollar bill. His uncle would need the money for the dinner, he figured, money and a lot of luck if he wanted to catch Vicky.

Uncle winked at Hector and whispered, "You're a great nephew. We'll meet you out front in ten minutes."

"*Simón,*" Hector exclaimed and wheeled away with Mando shrugging into his coat.

They left the restaurant, toothpicks in their mouths, and crossed the parking lot in a hurry because the night had grown cold. A puddle was stiff with ice and mud. A wind stirred a broken kite hanging from a telephone wire. Even the pigeons, clustered near a steamy grate, hunkered together like a gang, warbling. Hector and Mando walked into the mall, rubbing their hands and complaining of the cold. But soon they shook off the cold and sauntered aimlessly through the mall, window shopping.

"My uncle seems pretty silly," Hector said at the Wherehouse Record Store. Two girls had caught their eyes, and they watched them float by, packages under their arms.

"He's in love, *ese.*"

"Yeah, I know," Hector agreed, "but Mando, he kept telling Vicky how he liked her dress. Even the buttons. It was embarrassing."

They entered a Footlocker that was blaring a song. Hector tried on a pair of Reeboks with an air pump and walked around the store, shoelaces dragging. The shoes fit comfortably, and he would have bought them except that his pockets held only a comb, a pencil, and a pinch of sunflower seeds — nothing worth bartering.

They left the Footlocker. Hector asked Mando, "Do you think those guys will really get us?"

"*Quién sabes*, Hector. If my older brother wasn't in the service, he'd help us out. He'd get his army friends."

"I thought his friends were in prison."

"Some of 'em. Some are in the army or at City College."

They walked from store window to store window in silence. The girls they had seen earlier were in view. They were sharing a cotton candy, pulling at the feathery hairdo of pinkish candy.

"It was weird," Hector said vaguely. "He was right *there*, in the doctor's house."

"I wonder why he didn't grab us then? I would have if I had been him."

Hector touched his throat. He still remembered the mean stare and the words, "It's your turn to have your neck broken." He touched the back of his neck, the softest bone in his lean body, and shivered at the thought. "I'm glad that he didn't tear into us right there. We would have missed a good dinner."

They left the mall and were starting back to

the restaurant when they heard a honk. For a second, Hector thought it was *them*. But he looked past the shining headlights and saw that it was Uncle's Ford, a belch of steam rising from under the hood. Uncle got out of the car and ran up to Hector and Mando.

"Listen, I need your help," he whispered, looking back at the Ford where Vicky sat dabbing lipstick on her mouth. His face was flushed and his eyes were wild with excitement. It had been months since he had had a date, and the first with two boys looking on. "Vicky digs me. She says I look like Carlos Santana."

"You don't look like Santana."

"That's not the point," Uncle said. "I'm gonna drop you guys off at the apartment and go back to her place for coffee."

"Come on, Unc, we weren't born yesterday — or the day before," Hector said.

"All right, I'm going for a glass of wine. Be mellow." He paused for a second and waited for the boys to show a little sympathy. Surely, he thought, they understood something about love.

Hector and Mando looked at each other. They shrugged their shoulders and said, "Okay with us."

"I won't be long," he said. "And Hector, thanks for dropping that ten on me."

"It was a twenty, Unc."

"Oh, yeah, that's right — the twenty." He looked back at the car. Vicky was now playing with her hair. "She's really cute and smart."

They piled into the rattling Ford and started back to the apartment listening to country-western music on the car radio. The song was about a tumbleweed that blew from New Mexico to Oregon. All of them laughed and ridiculed the song.

"I remember a dog that walked from Sacramento to his home in Merced," Vicky told Hector and Mando. "I wrote an article about him."

"*¿De veras?*" Hector asked, his head propped between Vicky's and Uncle's shoulders.

Vicky told them the story. She said the owners thought that the dog was asleep in the back seat of their car and pulled out of a McDonald's with burgers and fries but no dog. Instead while the owners were inside McDonald's the dog had jumped out the window and taken up with a boy on the slide. The boy then sneaked the dog into his own car, where he was passed from one child to the next and squeezed like a toy. They brought the dog to Sacramento. He escaped there from the family and ventured back to Merced, through pastures and fields, subdivisions, business parks, busy streets, and freeways.

"Didn't they make a movie about that dog?" Hector asked.

"Could be," Vicky said and then turned to Uncle and, touching his sleeve, said, "I hope you're not upset about the article running in the newspaper." She was referring to the column, "Today's Youth."

"No, not at all," Uncle lied. "It made the boys celebrities."

Hector and Mando looked at each other and mouthed the word "Celebrities?"

They rounded the corner where the rear window had fallen out. The glass glistened like spilled treasure. Hector pointed at the glass and Uncle said vaguely, "I wonder why it fell out."

Uncle pulled into the driveway of his apartment. The boys got out, and Uncle Julio walked between them to the door, his hands squeezing their shoulders and instructing them, "Don't open the door for anyone. *¿Entienden?*"

"Don't worry, Unc," Hector said. "I know self-defense. I'm invincible."

"I'm gonna break that ugly one's face," Mando growled, jabbing at the night air. "I'll make him so ugly that when his mom sees him, she's gonna jump from a building."

Uncle sighed and said, "Maybe I shouldn't go." He looked back at the idling car, where

Vicky sat waiting. But the yin and yang of desire pulled on his heart.

"Nah, Unc — go! Don't worry about us."

Uncle sighed even deeper and let out a ghost of breath that hung in the cold air. He shook his head. He opened the front door and then he wagged his finger at them. He warned them, "Okay, but don't answer the door. You got it?"

They gave Uncle a thumbs-up sign. Uncle patted them on their backs and hurried back to the car, his bum leg giving him no problem.

Hector and Mando walked up the stairwell, feeling the walls because the apartment lights were off. At the top of the stairs, Hector felt around for a light switch. He flicked it on, and for a second he thought that maybe the robbers would be standing there grinning. Instead, he was staring at Uncle's pants on a coat hanger, the pants that he'd spilled coffee on and had washed in the kitchen sink.

Hector turned on the floor furnace and then checked the message machine. He poked a finger at the replay button and listened to, "Is Rick there! I wanna talk to Rick! I'm gettin' tired of him not calling!"

Hector and Mando dropped to their knees and rolled on the ground with laughter. The woman seemed desperate. The second beep sounded and a voice said "Hi, *mi'jo.*" It took Hector a moment to recognize his mother's voice. "I hope you and Mando are having fun. I'm okay. Chorizo got in another fight with the neighbor's cat. He lost . . ." The message droned on like a bee and ended with a warning for them to be nice or else. They waited for the third message and when the beep sounded there was a series of heh, heh, heh, heh laughs, which spooked Hector. There was just that eerie laughter and nothing more. Full of anger, Hector punched the message machine and snapped, "Okay, clown face. Come and get us!"

CHAPTER 16

"That's a stupid song," Freddie sneered. "How can a tumbleweed go from New Mexico to Oregon." He snapped off the radio, crossed his arms, and then uncrossed them to wipe the fogged window with his handkerchief. "Country music's getting so ridiculous."

"Garth Brooks is good," argued Huey.

"Good for what? Did you see how he wears his hat over his face? Can't even see his teeth when he sings."

They were parked in front of Uncle's apartment, the engine on and warm air circulating. They had been waiting forty minutes, eating peanuts and drinking Dr Pepper.

"Yeah, we'll take care of the kids," Freddie mused.

"We gonna hurt 'em?" Huey asked. "I don't feel like cryin' again, Freddie. I'm in a pretty good mood."

"Nah, we won't hurt 'em, or if we do, we

116

make it painless, like when you stomp a frog."

"I can't do that either, Freddie."

"Don't be a scaredy cat. They got the photos, and we got to get 'em. Now shut up!" Freddie was in a bad mood. He had sat there nearly an hour, loading up on junk food, and what he wanted more than anything was a hot bath with mountains of bubbles.

They waited in silence, the glow of the dashboard lights on their faces, which were lit up with shadows under their eyes.

When Julio's Ford rattled up the street and squeaked into the driveway, Freddie turned off their engine. They waited for three minutes. Then Freddie said, "Let's get it over with. I don't want to miss the Olympics."

They got out of their stolen Oldsmobile, the icy night hitting them like a brick. They shuddered, complained of the cold, and crossed the street, where they leaned their faces between a hedge. Freddie saw the uncle huddle around the two boys, pat them on the back, and usher them inside the house. The uncle returned to the Ford, where a woman sat.

"He's dropping off the kids," Freddie chuckled. "What could be more perfect?"

"If the kids dropped dead right on the spot," Huey said, surprised by his outburst.

"That's the way to think," Freddie said, patting his shoulder roughly. "Good for you."

The Ford turned around, its headlights sweeping across the lawn, and rattled out of the driveway. Once the car was out of sight, Freddie and Huey entered the yard, chuckling.

CHAPTER 17

Hector rubbed his sore knuckles. The telephone message machine was harder than he had thought. He picked it up and, turning it over like a turtle, discovered that its face was cracked.

"Uh-oh," Hector said as he raised the receiver to his ear. The telephone was dead. Instead of the long buzz, he heard a faraway ocean sound with a lightning charge of static. He checked the plug: the line was plugged into its socket. He pressed a series of numbers: nothing but a faraway sound like the ocean. He gave Mando a sorrowful look and remarked, "We're doomed, *ese*. If those guys show up."

Mando placed the telephone to his ear. His index finger jumped on his telephone number in Los Angeles. The sound of ocean carried through the wire to his ear. Mando dropped the telephone, the cord corkscrewing to the floor.

"You broke it, *carnal*," Mando said.

Hector pressed the message machine and a

slow, moaning heh, heh, heh of laughter bounced off the apartment walls. The laughter made Hector shudder and Mando bite a fingernail from fear. Hector smacked the message machine again and banged it against the wall.

Hector walked over to the window that looked onto the chiropractor's house. A yellow light was on in the kitchen and a column of smoke was rising from the chimney. Hector could make out music — the faint squeak of violins and an operatic voice that sounded like choking. He wished he had stayed in Los Angeles; wished he'd never said to his mother, "I'm dead bored." Right now, he and Mando could be playing soccer at the community center or kicking around the city with a fistful of sunflower seeds, bellies sloshing soda.

Hector sighed, pounded his scraped fist into his palm, and threw himself on the couch. He thought for a moment, thumbnail to his mouth. He thought of Bertha Sanchez, knowing that no one could be hit by her and still live a normal life. He would give anything, his front teeth included, if only Bertha were on their side.

Hector got up and scurried into the bathroom. In the shower Uncle's T-shirts and underwear, all gray as cement, hung drying among strips of negatives curled like vines. Hector searched for the negatives of the robbers. Once he found them, he unclipped them from the hanger and returned to the living room, where he raised them to the lamp: the ugly mug of the robber with thinning hair glared at him angrily.

"Let me see," said Mando as he sat next to Hector. He winced as he studied the negatives.

"Listen, Mando, we're not in danger. I mean, are they really gonna come and get us? No way, dude." Hector pounded his fist into his hands and jabbed at the air. He was trying hard to convince his friend. "There are laws against adults hurting minors."

"There are?"

"Yeah, sure there are."

"But Hector, these guys don't care about laws." Mando's voice sounded like the voice of a scolded child. When Mando lowered his head, the shadows under his eyes deepened. He stood up and paced the living room. He kicked a brown bean bag chair and asked, "How we gonna get out? We're upstairs."

Hector didn't answer Mando at first. He surveyed the apartment. The only door leading out was the front door. There were plenty of windows to jump from, although the second-story jump would probably hobble them.

"We're faster, and we're smarter," Hector finally said. Mando wasn't satisfied with that answer. He kept pacing the living room, head down.

Hector picked up the negatives and studied the images. He concluded that the robbers — the one pictured in the negative at least — were out of shape. They couldn't possibly catch him or Mando, he thought to himself. "Listen, if they come after us we'll run behind Dr. Femur's house and meet at the corner where Uncle's window fell out." Hector waved Mando over to the window. He pointed and said, "We'll go behind those trees and — " Hector stopped abruptly when he saw two figures waving at them: Freddie Bork and Huey "Crybaby" Walker, both smiling and laughing "heh, heh, heh." Hector looked at the negative, then at Freddie, whose laughter was jiggling his belly. Three times he looked from the negatives to the men outside and then backed away from the window. He turned to Mando and said, "This is it, Mando. Just throw something if they get in."

Immediately there was a bang, a big shoulder bouncing against the front door. Hector rushed to the kitchen, looking for something to throw at them. He picked up the salad dressing hoping the vinegar would sting the robbers' eyeballs. He ran down the steps and, after unscrewing the cap from the bottle, opened the peephole.

The banging stopped. "Listen, you've got the wrong kids."

"We've got the right ones," Freddie growled. "Ain't you the straight-A students?"

"No way, we only get C's," Hector answered back.

"The paper said you were a straight-A student."

"Listen, I'll tell you where the negatives are if that's what you're after. Honest, they're not here." The bottle of salad dressing was poised.

"Where are they?" Freddie edged toward the peephole and looked in.

"Right here," Hector said and sloshed Freddie's bloodshot eye with the Super Bowl salad dressing.

"What — !" Freddie had one palm pressed against his eye as his other hand dug in his pocket for a handkerchief. Hector sniffed a sweet pungent scent and looked at the bottle drooling an oily liquid. He touched his finger to the lip of the bottle and smelled it. The smell was sweet, and the taste sweeter than he expected when he raked his finger across his lower front teeth.

Hector put his eye to the peephole and saw Freddie licking his fingers, nodding his head and saying, "It has a pleasant tang, but maybe a little too much sugar." But when Freddie raised his gaze and focused on the door, he became menacingly enraged. He hiked up his pants. He growled to himself as he lowered his shoulder and charged.

Hector moved away and grimaced when Freddie's body banged with a terrifying noise. The door held. The door held a second and third time.

Hector retreated to the top of the stairs. Mando was on his knees trying to piece together the telephone.

"What are you doin'?" Hector asked.

"Tryin' to call home."

"Forget it, Mando."

Mando sighed and rose to his feet, a screwdriver in his hand.

Hector searched the apartment for something to slow down the robbers. He spotted an empty aquarium, which was brimming with marbles. "Help me," Hector told Mando. Together they hoisted the aquarium into their arms and brought it to the stairwell. Hector tossed a handful of marbles down, and they ricocheted against the sides of the walls as they clacked down the steps. He then moved Uncle's bowling ball into position, their atomic weapon if they needed one.

When the banging stopped, Hector became suspicious. From the window he searched the yard. He couldn't see or hear anything. He could make out, however, the choking voice coming from Dr. Femur's house. The opera singer was letting loose her cavernous lungs.

Mando hunkered down next to Hector and asked, "Do you see anything?"

Just as Hector answered "No," Freddie's face appeared out of the dark. It was shining in the glare of the streetlight. He was hanging on the telephone wire, moving hand over hand toward the apartment.

Hector and Mando shot up to their feet. Hector's eyes fell upon Uncle's cane, propped in the corner. He snatched it up, and returned to the window. Mando picked up the answering machine.

Freddie swung hand over hand toward the apartment. He was laughing and taunting, "Okay, you straight-A students, here comes the new teacher." Freddie was now under the eaves, his feet searching for a foothold on the ledge. "What's the capital of Egypt, my little friends?" Freddie continued to taunt.

From below, Huey bellowed, "Cairo."

Freddie answered, "That's good Huey. But let's give the boys a chance."

Hector opened the window and announced, "I'm making a citizen's arrest."

Freddie laughed and, with a meaty hand, grabbed the eave and pulled himself onto the ledge, where he tottered for a moment. But he regained his balance. He kicked the window and glass crashed to the ground. "Oops," Freddie laughed, "I hope your uncle has renter's insurance. Now what's the capital of Poland?"

"Warsaw," Hector answered and poked the curled end of Uncle's cane under Freddie's chin. Freddie fell backwards, arms flailing and screaming. But he managed to grab the telephone wire. Hector jutted the cane out the window and started poking Freddie's underarms, tickling them as the cane ran like a saw under his arm. Freddie laughed long and hard, causing his pants to wiggle down a bit. Freddie dropped, his fall broken by a hedge and a climbing rosebush. He got up slowly, brushing his hands free of mud, muttering as Huey helped him to his feet. He pulled a rose thorn from the tip of his nose.

"What's the capital of California?" Freddie asked angrily.

"For you, San Quentin, *ese*," Hector snapped smartly.

Mando threw the message machine, which crashed on Huey's foot. Huey leaped about, cussing, as the machine on its last juice moaned, "Is Rick there! I wanna talk to Rick!"

Freddie poked his shoe at the message machine and muttered to himself, "Who's Rick?"

Returning to glare at the boys, he yelled, "We're not done with you!"

The pounding started again on the front door, a double whammy of bodies that splintered open the door. Huey kicked the door and Freddie entered asking, "Okay, what's the capital of Argentina?"

"Lima," Mando answered.

"You're not straight-A students. It's Buenos Aires," Freddie growled through his panting. A trickle of blood ran from the tip of his nose. His hair was mussed and his eyes were more bloodshot than ever. "See what's wrong with today's youth?" he asked Huey. "They don't know their geography. They don't know how to show respect to their elders."

Freddie and Huey raced up the stairwell, legs churning. Hector and Mando turned over the aquarium, and the marbles spilled with a great clatter. Freddie and Huey slipped and landed face forward on the steps. They cried out and tumbled and rolled to the bottom. They lay still for a second, a silence filling in, and slowly moaned back to life. They looked up, eyes spinning groggily.

"That was pretty good," Huey muttered. With his hand on his chin, he opened and closed his jaw like a drawer.

"I hate these kids," Freddie said as he rose to

his feet and rubbed the small of his back. He pointed a finger and growled, "Go ahead, make my day."

"All right," Hector snapped and let the bowling bowl go. It bounced off one side of the stairwell and then the other, gathering momentum.

They didn't watch to see what happened, but they heard screams and a body slapping to the floor. Hector and Mando retreated in a hurry to Uncle's bedroom. They moved a dresser in front of the door and then the mattress. Hector spied Uncle's Nikon on the nightstand. He grabbed it, ripped off the lens cap, and brought it to his eye and focused.

"We could jump from the window," Mando suggested.

They peeked out of the window and shivered at the thought. On this side of the house, the drop was more than three stories onto a concrete patio. At Dr. Femur's house the music was now even louder, a choking and wailing of opera singers.

"I got an idea," Hector said, snapping his fingers. "We'll hide and when they come in, we'll blind them."

"What, with more salad dressing?"

"No, this," Hector said and, aiming at Mando, pressed the button of the camera. The room filled with a bright flash that made Mando stagger, rubbing his eyes.

"*Híjole*, I can't see anything," Mando cried. He stretched out his hands. "Help me, Hector."

"You'll be okay in a sec'," Hector said and advanced the film. He then spotted a pile of old record albums, the ones that his mother told him to return to his uncle. "Then we'll smash 'em with Santana!"

Hector searched the room and his eyes fell on a tape recorder. "Hey, Mando, we can even record our own funeral."

"That's not funny," Mando said.

Freddie and Huey were now at the door, cooing, "Boys, we're not here to hurt you. We just want to talk. Be friends, you know, maybe become partners." There was a silence and then Freddie continued. "You like money, don't you? We'll split what we have."

Hector had turned on their tape recorder and, taunting Freddie, "Hey, dude, listen to yourself. You're corrupting Today's Youths." He played it back for Freddie, who was furious. "I'm going to tear you to pieces, punk," he growled.

Hector laughed.

"Don't get him mad, Hector," Mando warned.

"Yeah, you're right."

When the pounding began on the door, Hector

turned off the overhead light and picked up a five-pound weight from the closet and started beating the light switch. He beat it until the switch was broken. The robbers would have to search for them in the dark. Next, he moved Uncle's Mexican flag from the wall to the middle of the floor.

Mando drew the drapes over the window. The bedroom was now completely dark. Hector and Mando hunkered down together. Their hearts boomed as the door slowly gave way and the dresser fell over like a beast. Huey pushed an arm through, then a leg, and finally his whole body. Freddie followed. He was breathing hard as he stepped over the mattress. They walked in the dark, bumping against each other. Freddie mumbled, "Come on, kids, make life simple for us."

For a moment, Freddie and Huey stood motionless, trying to pick up the sound of breathing. Hector felt for sure that they could hear their heartbeats. Hector touched the Nikon around his neck and prayed that it would work.

When Huey took a step, Hector felt a book on the floor. He tossed it in the far corner, which made Freddie and Huey spin around and start after the sound. When they stepped on the flag Hector yanked it hard, sending the intruders sprawling. As they fell backwards Hector and

Mando jumped up, their hands loaded with records. They pummeled them with records, which cracked and shattered on their heads.

But when Freddie staggered to his feet, Hector raised the camera, aimed and shot a blinding flash at Freddie. His hands went to his eyes, and Hector smacked him one.

Freddie again staggered to his feet, and Hector flashed the camera at him. Mando kicked him in the shin and Huey, who was starting to cry, crumbled to the floor.

Hector, remembering a Bruce Lee movie, screamed like a monkey and slammed his fist into Freddie's solar plexus. Freddie doubled over, moaning, "I hate kids, especially these two . . ." Hector gave him a karate chop on the back of his neck.

Freddie dropped like a bundle of laundry and Hector searched the closet for something to tie Freddie up with. He found a pair of pants — Uncle's old hippie bell-bottoms. He jumped on Freddie, who was out like a light, and tied his arms behind his back while Mando used a rope of exposed film to tie up blubbering Huey.

Hector looked up scared when he heard hurried footsteps climbing the stairs.

"Don't tell me there are three of 'em," Hector said to Mando.

Hector rose to his feet, his heart thumping like

the back legs of a rabbit. For a moment, he thought of Bertha Sanchez and gathered all the strength in his body. This is it, he thought.

When a figure showed up in the doorway and stumbled over the mattress, Hector flashed the camera and without even asking, "Hey, who are you, dude?," he punched the guy in the stomach.

"*Híjole,*" the voice groaned while he dropped to his knees.

"Ooops," Hector said as he turned around and searched for Mando in the dark. "It's Uncle."

CHAPTER 18

Uncle rummaged through his closet for his old black telephone. It was there, languishing among his dusty baseball trophies. As Uncle plugged in the phone and dialed 911, his gaze remained locked on Freddie and Huey who were tied on the floor, moaning. He explained the scene to the dispatcher, hung up, and helped Hector and Mando locate an electrical outlet for a lamp they had moved into the bedroom.

Hector, still breathing hard from the excitement, turned on the lamp. A yellow light revealed the prone bodies of Freddie and Huey, their legs and arms bound in rags and Uncle's old bell-bottom pants.

"I'm sorry I left you guys alone," Uncle apologized. "I called you from Vicky's. I didn't get an answer, so I knew something was up."

"It's okay," Hector said. He bent down and picked up the broken pieces of a Santana album. "Sorry, Unc."

"Hey, no problem. It had a bunch of scratches anyway."

Huey turned his face to Hector. Tears were running down his face, and Hector felt sorry for him. He bent down closely and asked, "Are you hurtin' or something?"

Huey shook his head. He sobbed, "I'm going to miss the ski jumping."

"And it's all your fault," Freddie said as he turned his wincing face in Hector's direction. Unlike Huey, who was all sorrow and dirty tears, Freddie was alive and kicking with anger. He tried to scramble to his knees.

"It's the other way around," Uncle corrected as he pushed Freddie back to the floor with the heel of his shoe. "You've got no right to rob an armored car."

"Sure we did. We were broke."

"I'm broke too," Uncle said.

"Me too," Mando said. "Always have been."

"Then let's make a deal," Freddie suggested with enthusiasm. "We can all split the money — one-fifth for each of us broke guys."

"Forget it!" Hector snapped. "You ruined our vacation."

When the telephone rang, the three of them jumped and yelled, "¡Ay, Dios!" On the fifth ring, Hector picked it up and heard a voice scream, "Is Rick there! I want to talk with Rick?"

Hector lowered the receiver onto the cradle. "Wrong number," he told Uncle and Mando.

From a distance, they could make out the wail of police sirens. Hector could picture the police cars, gumballs turning and tires squealing around the corners. He pictured clean-shaven policemen, jaws square and tense, their revolvers heavy at their sides, the angel of death in each faceless bullet.

"Help me with this dresser?" Uncle asked. Shaking his finger at Freddie and Huey, he growled, "You two stay put! Or I'll feed you to Hector and Mando."

Hector snapped out of his police daydream when he heard his name. With Mando, he righted the dresser and moved it against the wall. They tugged the mattress back onto the bed, which gave Uncle a reason to change his sheets. The sheets were brown, same as all the furniture in the house. They were sweeping up when they heard the police cars, tires screaming.

The three of them looked out the broken window that faced Dr. Femur's house. The music was still playing, the opera singer still choking on something.

Hector looked up at the clock: 11:47. "Time flies when you're throwing *pleitos*," he said.

The police got slowly out of their cars, fitting their nightsticks on their belts, and walked, not ran, up the stairs. To Hector's surprise, they were not clean shaven. Their faces were heavy and tired, and one was chewing a wad of gum.

"In there," Uncle said, hooking a thumb toward the bedroom.

The officers moved slowly toward the bedroom, but when they discovered two men tied up in there, they became excited. Their sense of duty even got a bit crazy when they learned that it was the two men involved in the armored car heist. They handcuffed them and yanked them to their feet. Huey's face was wet with tears. Freddie's face was dark with anger. He mumbled, "I hate these kids," and the police pushed them from the bedroom to the waiting cars below.

Uncle explained the events to one officer, and Hector and Mando explained to another. The police stayed for a while, taking notes and confiscating Uncle's negatives. They even took Uncle's Nikon and the message machine which had recorded Freddie's threats.

"Come on, man, my camera?" Uncle yelled, his hands running through his hair. "It's my bread and butter!"

"You can pick it up tomorrow," one officer answered and, looking around before he left the apartment, added, "This place is a mess."

Uncle flopped his arms at his side and shook

his head as he led the officer out of the apartment. He returned, smiling. The officer had returned the camera, minus the film.

Hector and Mando swept up the hallway of marbles and broken glass, and hauled the smashed aquarium to the side of the apartment. Uncle called Vicky and told her what had happened. He hung up and touched the front of his shirt. "Man, that's funny. My heart's beating hard just telling the story."

Fifteen minutes later, Vicky was running up the steps in her high heels. Her face was strained with worry as she asked, "Are you all right? Hector? Mando?"

"*Simón*," Mando answered. "Except I gotta cold." He ran a finger under his nose and searched his pocket for a Kleenex.

She gave Hector and Mando a hug and then held open her palm and asked, "Whose marbles are these?"

"Ah, well, they're mine," Uncle said embarrassed. "From the aquarium."

Vicky pressed a handful into Uncle's palm, and put down a paper bag that held coffee, bagels, and cream cheese. Vicky looked around the apartment. "You must really like brown, Julio?"

"*Pues sí*. It's the color of *raza*, *qué no*," Uncle said, shrugging his shoulders.

The boys bit their lips, not wanting to let on

that Unc's ex-wife took off with everything that wasn't brown.

Vicky poured them coffee and cut the bagels in half, slapping them with a layer of cream cheese. They ate their midnight snack standing up, Hector giving Vicky and his uncle a blow by blow account of what happened.

"Yeah, I tied the *vato* into a pretzel," Mando bragged.

"*¡Simón!* And I karate chopped the other one," Hector said. He yelled and chopped the air with his open-hand palm.

Mando turned to Vicky and said, "You shoulda seen us."

Vicky put down her bagel. She was no longer hungry. She sat the boys on the couch, and cooed soothing words at Hector and Mando. "You're such brave boys," Vicky said, smoothing their hair. Hector and Mando beamed like babies in her arms while Uncle sat in a chair watching jealously. She sat with the boys and told them repeatedly that she was sorry about the "Today's Youth" article.

The four of them — Hector, Mando, Uncle, and Vicky — stayed up all night. They cleaned up the house and patched the two broken windows with cardboard. They listened to Uncle's old hippie music, danced, and then when they remembered that there was a five thousand dollar reward, they sat at the kitchen table drawing up plans for a real vacation.

"You been to Hawaii?" Hector asked his uncle.

"One time."

"Was it fun?"

"Yeah, once I got out of the hospital. I broke my collarbone while surfing."

"Forget Hawaii. Let's go to Mexico, to *la playa*," Mando suggested. He stuffed his face with another toothy bite of a bagel.

"Yeah, let's all go to Acapulco," Hector said dreamily.

"You mean me, too?" Vicky asked, winking at Uncle. "I have vacation time coming up."

"*Pues sí*," Mando said.

"Yeah, of course," Hector added.

Uncle rested his hand over Vicky's. Vicky smiled and turned her hand over, so that their fingers became interlaced.

The four of them dreamed of the beach-front hotel with the Pacific waves breaking at their feet.

GLOSSARY

amigo — friend

ándale — let's go

ay — (exclamation) oh

¡ay, Dios! — oh God!

buenas tardes — good afternoon

¡cállate! — be quiet!

cálmesen — calm down

carnal — blood brother, good friend

chále — no way

chamacos — kids

Chicano — Mexican-American

chingadasos — fierce fighting

cholo — low rider

cochino — pig

¿Cómo se llaman sus niños? — What are your boys' names?

de veras — really

en serio — seriously

¿entienden? — understand?

escuincles — little kids

ese — guy

hace mucho frío — it's cold

híjole — wow, gosh

hombres — men

huevos con chorizo — eggs with Mexican sausage

huevos con weenies — eggs with frankfurters

gatitos — kittens

gatos — cats

la playa — the seashore

laganas — dried mucus

loca — crazy girl

MEChA — student organization (Movimiento Estudiantil Chicano de Aztlan)

Mechista — a member of MEChA

mi'jo — (endearment) my son

mi darkroom es tu darkroom — my darkroom is your darkroom

mucho dinero — lots of money

mucho gusto — a pleasure

no sé — I don't know

novio — lover

¡órale! — all right!

panadería — bakery

pásen — come in

pleitos — punches

policía — police

precioso — precious

pronto — quickly

pues sí — of course

¿qué pasa? — what's happening?

¿qué no? — isn't that right?

quién — who

quién sabes — who knows

rayo — lightning bolt

raza — Latino people

ruca — girlfriend (slang)

señora — Mrs.

simón — okay, yes

su carnal de San Francisco — your friend from San Francisco

tío — uncle

tonto — idiot

vato loco — crazy dude

vatos — guys

vieja — old woman

ABOUT THE AUTHOR

GARY SOTO has received great praise for his books for young readers and adults, including *Local News*; *Baseball in April and Other Stories*; *Living up the Street*; and two collections of poetry, *A Fire in My Hands* and *Neighborhood Odes*. Mr. Soto has also produced three short films for Spanish-speaking children, *The Bike*; *Novio Boy*; and *Pool Party*, which won the American Library Association's Andrew Carnegie Medal for excellence in filmmaking.

Mr. Soto was born and raised in Fresno, California, and now teaches at the University of California at Berkeley. Like the boys in *Crazy Weekend*, he likes photography and is reluctant to fly in small planes.